INTRODUCING ISSUES WITH OPPOSING VIEWPOINTS®

Torture

Lauri S. Friedman, *Book Editor*

GREENHAVEN PRESS
A part of Gale, Cengage Learning

GALE
CENGAGE Learning™

Detroit • New York • San Francisco • New Haven, Conn • Waterville, Maine • London

GALE
CENGAGE Learning

Christine Nasso, *Publisher*
Elizabeth Des Chenes, *Managing Editor*

© 2011 Greenhaven Press, a part of Gale, Cengage Learning

Gale and Greenhaven Press are registered trademarks used herein under license.

For more information, contact:
Greenhaven Press
27500 Drake Rd.
Farmington Hills, MI 48331-3535
Or you can visit our Internet site at gale.cengage.com

Articles in Greenhaven Press anthologies are often edited for length to meet page requirements. In addition, original titles of these works are changed to clearly present the main thesis and to explicitly indicate the author's opinion. Every effort is made to ensure that Greenhaven Press accurately reflects the original intent of the authors. Every effort has been made to trace the owners of copyrighted material.

Cover image copyright © Phase4Photography/Shutterstock.com.

LIBRARY OF CONGRESS CATALOGING-IN-PUBLICATION DATA

Torture / Lauri S. Friedman, book editor.
   p. cm. -- (Introducing issues with opposing viewpoints)
  Includes bibliographical references and index.
  ISBN 978-0-7377-5203-8 (hardcover)
  1. Torture--United States. 2. Torture--Government policy--United States. 3. Torture--Moral and ethical aspects--United States. I. Friedman, Lauri S.
   HV8599.U6.T67 2011
   364.6'7--dc22

                                                          2011005638

Printed in the United States of America
1 2 3 4 5 6 7 15 14 13 12 11

Contents

Foreword

Indulging in a wide spectrum of ideas, beliefs, and perspectives is a critical cornerstone of democracy. After all, it is often debates over differences of opinion, such as whether to legalize abortion, how to treat prisoners, or when to enact the death penalty, that shape our society and drive it forward. Such diversity of thought is frequently regarded as the hallmark of a healthy and civilized culture. As the Reverend Clifford Schutjer of the First Congregational Church in Mansfield, Ohio, declared in a 2001 sermon, "Surrounding oneself with only like-minded people, restricting what we listen to or read only to what we find agreeable is irresponsible. Refusing to entertain doubts once we make up our minds is a subtle but deadly form of arrogance." With this advice in mind, Introducing Issues with Opposing Viewpoints books aim to open readers' minds to the critically divergent views that comprise our world's most important debates.

Introducing Issues with Opposing Viewpoints simplifies for students the enormous and often overwhelming mass of material now available via print and electronic media. Collected in every volume is an array of opinions that captures the essence of a particular controversy or topic. Introducing Issues with Opposing Viewpoints books embody the spirit of nineteenth-century journalist Charles A. Dana's axiom: "Fight for your opinions, but do not believe that they contain the whole truth, or the only truth." Absorbing such contrasting opinions teaches students to analyze the strength of an argument and compare it to its opposition. From this process readers can inform and strengthen their own opinions, or be exposed to new information that will change their minds. Introducing Issues with Opposing Viewpoints is a mosaic of different voices. The authors are statesmen, pundits, academics, journalists, corporations, and ordinary people who have felt compelled to share their experiences and ideas in a public forum. Their words have been collected from newspapers, journals, books, speeches, interviews, and the Internet, the fastest growing body of opinionated material in the world.

Introducing Issues with Opposing Viewpoints shares many of the well-known features of its critically acclaimed parent series, Opposing Viewpoints. The articles are presented in a pro/con format, allowing readers to absorb divergent perspectives side by side. Active reading questions preface each viewpoint, requiring the student to approach the material thoughtfully and carefully. Useful charts, graphs, and cartoons supplement each article. A thorough introduction provides readers with crucial background on an issue. An annotated bibliography points the reader toward articles, books, and websites that contain additional information on the topic. An appendix of organizations to contact contains a wide variety of charities, nonprofit organizations, political groups, and private enterprises that each hold a position on the issue at hand. Finally, a comprehensive index allows readers to locate content quickly and efficiently.

Introducing Issues with Opposing Viewpoints is also significantly different from Opposing Viewpoints. As the series title implies, its presentation will help introduce students to the concept of opposing viewpoints and learn to use this material to aid in critical writing and debate. The series' four-color, accessible format makes the books attractive and inviting to readers of all levels. In addition, each viewpoint has been carefully edited to maximize a reader's understanding of the content. Short but thorough viewpoints capture the essence of an argument. A substantial, thought-provoking essay question placed at the end of each viewpoint asks the student to further investigate the issues raised in the viewpoint, compare and contrast two authors' arguments, or consider how one might go about forming an opinion on the topic at hand. Each viewpoint contains sidebars that include at-a-glance information and handy statistics. A Facts About section located in the back of the book further supplies students with relevant facts and figures.

Following in the tradition of the Opposing Viewpoints series, Greenhaven Press continues to provide readers with invaluable exposure to the controversial issues that shape our world. As John Stuart Mill once wrote: "The only way in which a human being can make some approach to knowing the whole of a subject is by hearing what can be said about it by persons of every variety of opinion and studying all modes in which it can be looked at by every character of mind. No wise man ever acquired his wisdom in any mode but this." It is to this principle that Introducing Issues with Opposing Viewpoints books are dedicated.

Introduction

Debates about torture do not go on for long without one party introducing the "ticking time bomb" scenario, a moral hypothetical that goes as follows: Authorities have apprehended a terrorist who has critical information about an impending terror attack. Do they torture this person to prevent the attack?

The modern origins of the ticking time bomb scenario have been traced by political science professor Darius Rejali to the 1960 French novel *Les Centurions* by Jean Larteguy, which takes place during the French occupation of Algeria. In the book, a French soldier discovers a plot to explode bombs around the country after torturing an Algerian rebel. Lives are saved because of the soldier's actions.

More than a decade later, philosopher Michael Walzer addressed the issue in an article called "The Problem of Dirty Hands," published by the journal *Philosophy and Public Affairs*. Read mostly by the academic community, the ticking time bomb scenario became fodder for a more mainstream audience when it was the subject of an influential 1982 *Newsweek* article by philosopher Michael Levin. In this piece, Levin posited three hypothetical situations that, in his opinion, made torture "not merely permissible but morally mandatory."[1] In one, a terrorist has planted an atomic bomb in Manhattan; in another, a terrorist has planted bombs on an airplane; in the third, a terrorist has kidnapped a baby. In all three, Levin argues that torturing the terrorist is morally justifiable if it will produce information that can thwart the attacks. "Torturing the terrorist is unconstitutional? Probably," he writes. "But millions of lives surely outweigh constitutionality. Torture is barbaric? Mass murder is far more barbaric."[2] Levin concluded his article with this haunting prophecy: "Some day soon a terrorist will threaten tens of thousands of lives, and torture will be the only way to save them. We had better start thinking about this."[3]

Nearly thirty years after this chilling warning, the United States and its international allies find themselves a decade into a war on terror in which ticking time bomb scenarios are decidedly less hypothetical.

Terrorists have successfully detonated bombs or caused mass death in the September 11, 2001, attacks on the United States; the March 11, 2004, Madrid train bombings; the July 7, 2005, London subway bombings; the 2008 attack on Mumbai, India; and have attempted other such attacks, including the 2010 plot to bomb Times Square in New York City. With each successful or attempted attack, scholars, policy makers, and antiterrorism experts debate the wisdom and usefulness of the ticking time bomb scenario.

Like Levin and Walzer, lawyer and professor Alan Dershowitz is a key voice arguing that torturing a captured terrorist is a repugnant but necessary and morally justifiable act that can save innocent lives. Just months after the September 11 attacks, Dershowitz acknowledged that not only would American officials employ torture in the event a captured terrorist had information that could prevent an attack, but "the vast majority of Americans would expect the officers to engage in that time-tested technique for loosening tongues, notwithstanding our unequivocal treaty obligation never to employ torture, no matter how exigent the circumstances."[4]

Syndicated columnist and noted conservative commentator Charles Krauthammer agrees, and he argues that ticking time bomb scenarios are not just hypothetical. Krauthammer reports that in October 1994 Israeli soldiers brutalized a Palestinian terrorist involved in the capture of soldier Nachshon Waxman. The scheme worked: The terrorist gave up Waxman's location. Krauthammer reports that Yitzhak Rabin, then prime minister of Israel, said, "If we'd been so careful to follow [anti-torture guidelines], we would never have found out where Waxman was being held."[5]

But others argue that the ticking time bomb scenario does not justify the use of terror. Even under the above-mentioned circumstances, torture is never moral, they say. Torture opponents believe that torture threatens to lead a nation down a slippery slope that jeopardizes its standing in the world and actually invites more terrorism. As writer Gary Kamiya puts it, "As America struggles to win hearts and minds in the Arab/Muslim world, the use of torture is more harmful in the long run than any 'high-value' intelligence gained by its use."[6] Kamiya and others argue that the best prevention against terrorism is not torturing people but preventing them from becoming terrorists in the first place, which involves projecting an image of America as just, fair, and moral.

Others go a step further and reject claims that the ticking time bomb scenario is anything more than hypothetical. Citing evidence that torture produces no valuable information, or worse, untrue or otherwise unreliable information, opponents of torture say ticking time bomb scenarios are inventions used by authority figures to manipulate otherwise moral people into supporting an unequivocally immoral act. As columnist Daniel Froomkin puts it, "The ticking time bomb scenario only exists in two places: On TV and in the dark fantasies of power-crazed and morally deficient authoritarians. In real life, things are never that certain."[7] Historian Alfred W. McCoy, agrees, saying that under close inspection, the main assumption inherent in the ticking time bomb scenario is faulty: "The probability that a terrorist might be captured after concealing a ticking nuclear bomb in Times Square and that his captors would somehow recognize his significance is phenomenally slender."[8]

In 2008, more than nineteen thousand citizens in nineteen countries were polled on their opinion of the ticking time bomb scenario, and most of them agreed with McCoy and Kamiya. In fourteen of the nineteen countries, the majority of citizens did not think torture was acceptable even if it would save innocent lives. Citizens of Spain, Great Britain, and France were most likely to reject such a scenario, with 82 percent of them saying that they do not support torture under any circumstance. Majorities in Mexico (73 percent) China (66 percent), the Palestinian Territories (66 percent), Poland (62 percent), and Indonesia (61 percent) also said they would not support the use of torture, even if lives could be saved as a result.

Whether effective, justifiable, or realistic, the ticking time bomb scenario is sure to remain a centerpiece of any debate about torture as long as the war on terror continues. This and other issues surrounding torture—such as whether it violates American values, and what interrogation methods qualify as torture—are among the many debates presented in *Introducing Issues with Opposing Viewpoints: Torture.* Pro/con article pairs expose readers to the basic debates surrounding torture and encourage them to make their own decisions about what US policy should be on this compelling topic.

Notes

1. Michael Levin, "The Case for Torture," *Newsweek*, June 7, 1982.
2. Michael Levin, "The Case for Torture."
3. Michael Levin, "The Case for Torture."
4. Alan Dershowitz, "Want to Torture? Get a Warrant," *San Francisco Chronicle*, January 22, 2002. www.sfgate.com/cgi-bin/article.cgi?file=/chronicle/archive/2002/01/22/ED5329.DTL
5. Quoted in Charles Krauthammer, "Torture Foes Twist the Truth: Ticking Time Bomb Scenarios Are Real," *New York Daily News*, May 14, 2009. www.nydailynews.com/opinions/2009/05/15/2009-05-15_torture_foes_twist_the_truth_.html.
6. Gary Kamiya, "Torture Works Sometimes—But It's Always Wrong," Salon.com, April 23, 2009. www.salon.com/news/opinion/kamiya/2009/04/23/torture.
7. Dan Froomkin, "Krauthammer's Asterisks," *Washington Post*, May 1, 2009. http://voices.washingtonpost.com/white-house-watch/torture/krauthammers-asterisks.html.
8. Alfred W. McCoy, "The Myth of the Ticking Time Bomb," Alternet.org, September 14, 2006. www.alternet.org/rights/41648/?page=1.

Chapter 1

Is Torture Ever Justified?

Under what circumstances torture should be used is the subject of much debate.

Viewpoint 1

Torture Is Sometimes Justified

Berl Falbaum

"Torture, as abhorrent a practice as it is, needs to be part of this nation's policy."

In the following viewpoint, Berl Falbaum argues that torture is justified because its use can save innocent lives. He discusses a classic "ticking time bomb" scenario, in which officials have captured a terrorist who knows about an impending attack that will kill thousands. In Falbaum's opinion, it is acceptable to torture this person to get him to reveal details of the attack in order to prevent it. Falbaum argues that had torture been part of US policy, the September 11, 2001, terrorist attacks might have been prevented. For all of these reasons, Falbaum believes torture should be a part of US policy and used sparingly when necessary to save American lives. Falbaum is a former political reporter who teaches journalism at Wayne State University.

AS YOU READ, CONSIDER THE FOLLOWING QUESTIONS:

1. Who is Mohamed Atta and how does he factor into the author's argument?
2. What about Senator John McCain's remarks on torture does Falbaum disagree with?
3. Falbaum poses a question to readers at the end of the viewpoint. What is this question? Do you agree with Falbaum that the likely answer is no?

Berl Falbaum, "Torture Sometimes a Necessary Evil," *Oakland Press,* April 7, 2010. Reprinted by permission.

Let us assume that the U.S. captures an enemy spy who has knowledge of a nuclear attack on a major American city that would kill hundreds of thousands of people.

Should the U.S. torture the spy to obtain the information and save a U.S. city?

Torture Could Have Prevented 9/11

Too far fetched? Not really, given that we will see a proliferation of nuclear weapons in the future, particularly in the hands of terrorists and nations which support terrorism.

But if some believe the nuclear scenario is too unrealistic, let's try this one: The U.S. arrested Mohamed Atta, the leader in the 9/11 attack, before the deadly planes flew into New York's World Trade Center Towers.

Surveillance video shows 9/11 hijacker Mohamed Atta, right, pass through Portland, Maine, airport security and board American Airlines Flight 11, which he then flew into the World Trade Center.

Most Americans Think Torture Is Justified

A 2009 poll found that the majority of Americans think the use of torture against suspected terrorists is either often or sometimes justified.

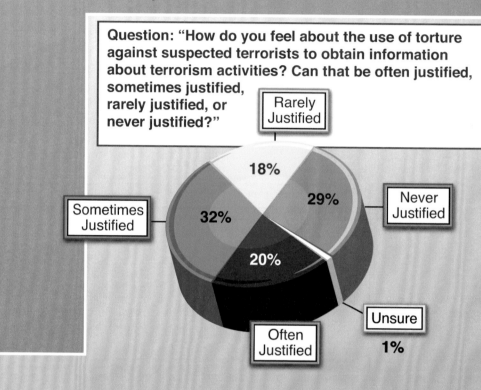

Question: "How do you feel about the use of torture against suspected terrorists to obtain information about terrorism activities? Can that be often justified, sometimes justified, rarely justified, or never justified?"

- Rarely Justified: 18%
- Never Justified: 29%
- Sometimes Justified: 32%
- Often Justified: 20%
- Unsure: 1%

Taken from: AP-GfK Poll conducted by GfK Roper Public Affairs & Media, May 28–June 1, 2009.

In his pockets, they found information regarding the planned attacks. Should the U.S. have tortured Atta to try and save 3,000 lives?

Hardly too unrealistic because many critics believed that the U.S. could have stopped the attacks with arrests of Atta and others who received pilot training in the U.S.

The answer to both these questions under the [Barack] Obama administration is a resounding "no," our opposition to torture is absolute. Our values are sacrosanct, the president said, if we hold true to them, we will be the stronger for it.

Torture Is Sometimes a Necessary Evil

In an ideal world, we would welcome and applaud Obama's eloquence and idealism. Indeed, torture is an ugly, inhumane, and despicable practice. Would that the world could rid itself of it. But. . . .

We, unfortunately, must act in accordance with reality not abstract concepts no matter how beautifully expressed. The fact is we live in a world where some do not share our commitment to the value for human life.

Even Sen. John McCain, who has made banning torture a major part of his political philosophy, addressed the issue of "rare" cases when much is at stake in an article in *Newsweek*. He wrote: "In such an urgent and rare instance, an interrogator might well try extreme measure to extract information that could save lives. Should he do so, and thereby save an American city or prevent another 9/11, authorities and the public would surely take this into account when judging his actions, and recognize the extremely dire situation which he confronted."

In other words, McCain would leave the judgment whether to torture to individual interrogators. That's hardly good public policy. It would be much more preferable to have a clearly defined policy on torture with appropriate controls to assure that the practice is not abused.

Perhaps we can require that interrogators would have to file petitions—like requests for wiretapping—with a special panel that would review the value of the information sought against the need to torture.

FAST FACT

The use of waterboarding, sleep deprivation, and other controversial interrogation techniques was recommended in a series of 2002 legal memos written by John Yoo, the former deputy assistant attorney general of the United States, and signed by Jay Bybee, a federal judge.

The United States Needs a Torture Policy

The point is torture, as abhorrent a practice as it is, needs to be part of this nation's policy. Yes, we must guard against abuses. Yes, the use of it needs to be carefully defined, and used as sparingly as possible.

To those who would object, here is one more question: Would they be willing to serve in combat under a commander—like Barack Obama—who tells his men he will never use torture even to elicit information that could save their lives? I did not think so.

EVALUATING THE AUTHOR'S ARGUMENTS:

Falbaum uses strong words to describe torture, saying it is "ugly," "inhumane," "despicable," and "abhorrent." Yet he ultimately supports its use. Given the fact that Falbaum supports torture, why do you think he chose to describe it using such negative words? In your opinion, does this detract from or enhance his argument?

Torture Is Never Justified

Walter Rodgers

In the following viewpoint, Walter Rodgers argues that torture is never justified. He interviews victims of torture to show that such treatment leaves long-lasting, horrific scars, and rarely yields credible or useful information. Rodgers believes the biggest problem with torture is that it lulls people into having a false sense of security. In his opinion, torture does not keep society safe, and it costs people—both victims and perpetrators—their humanity and decency. For these reasons, he concludes, torture is an inherently immoral act and its use is never justified.

Rodgers is a former senior international correspondent for CNN and writes a weekly column for the *Christian Science Monitor*, where this viewpoint was originally published.

"Torture, whatever its guise, is always immoral."

AS YOU READ, CONSIDER THE FOLLOWING QUESTIONS:
1. Who is "Yvette"? Which of the author's points does her story help prove true?
2. What does Rodgers suggest would work better than torture at getting Islamic terrorists to give up their plans?
3. What, according to the author, is the "fallacy of torture"?

Walter Rodgers, "Survivors Know Best: Torture Is Always Wrong," *Christian Science Monitor,* 2010. Reprinted by permission.

They live invisibly among us, 41,000 in the Washington area, half a million in the United States. They are survivors of horrific political torture. Unless they open their shirts, you detect few visible scars. "The mark of torture is more inside than out," says "Elena," a woman from Gabon who uses a wheelchair.

(Because everyone interviewed has living relatives in their native lands, all names have been changed at their request.)

Americans with no experience deceive themselves about torture. A friend told me that when the US tortured people it was somehow more humane.

But talk to torture victims at the annual gathering of the Torture Abolition and Survivors Support Coalition (TASSC) and they tell you that torture, whatever its guise, is always immoral.

"The Torturer Becomes the Terrorist"

In the early 1980s, Miguel was held prisoner for four years by the Marcos regime in the Philippines.[1] "Torture is always wrong," he says. "It uses terrorism to try to destroy terrorism. The torturer becomes the terrorist. You think you establish order by breaking the law."

Torture breaks people as well as the law. Yvette from Cameroon speaks slowly, vacantly, and without focus. One of the TASSC directors acknowledged that "her mind has yet to heal."

Yvette was tortured for belonging to a human rights defense group in Cameroon. Police were seeking information on political dissidents. "I was beaten continuously," she says. "They slapped my face and head for three days. I don't know how long I was unconscious." When Yvette regained consciousness, she was unable to walk for a week, her legs having been beaten with police batons.

"I think the pain will never stop," she says. "I still shake when I hear police sirens."

"Even in Washington, D.C.?" I ask.

"Yes. I feel like they're after me again."

---

1. Ferdinand Marcos was the Philippine president from 1965 to 1986. His presidency was marred by corruption, political repression, and human rights violations.

The International Reach of Torture

Some countries are investigating the US torture program and their governments' links to secret CIA prisons. In some cases the United States may have used secret prisons in other countries to torture suspected terrorists. In other cases it may have handed prisoners off from one country to another, a process known as rendition.

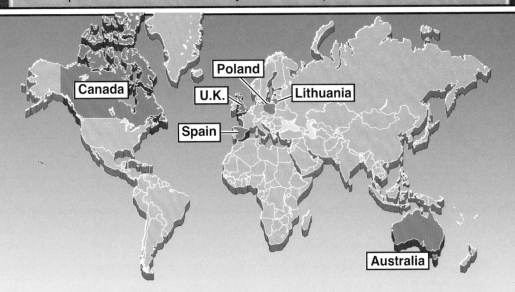

U.K.	Announced judicial inquiry after an Ethiopian national claimed British authorities knew he was being tortured by CIA but did not stop it.
Spain	Pending court case charges Bush administration officials with breaking international laws prohibiting torture.
Canada	Police are investigating the role of United States and Syrian officials in the imprisonment and torture of an innocent man.
Australia	A court ruled the government must respond to allegations that it was involved in the rendition and torture of a suspected terrorist.
Poland	Prosecutors may bring war crimes charges against former officials for allowing the CIA to operate a secret prison in Poland.
Lithuania	A government investigation found that Lithuanian intelligence services had helped the CIA operate no less than two secret prisons.

Taken from: McClatchy Washington Bureau, Graphic: Judy Treible, 2010.

The Tortured Either Lie or Keep Quiet

Perpetrators of torture share a common rationale: national security. "They tell you torture keeps your families safe and secure," says Miguel.

What about the Israeli argument—that torture can thwart a suicide bomber, or the American version: "What if Islamic terrorists planted a suitcase-sized nuclear bomb in New York City?"

I put that question to torture survivors. One asked, "Why torture anyone? Wouldn't you be better off finding an imam [an Islamic cleric] . . . to sit with the prisoner and let him persuade a suspect it's morally wrong to take innocent lives?"

Of the dozen survivors I interviewed, people from Asia, Africa, and the Middle East, each said torture doesn't work. In 2008, Mary from Uganda was beaten, gang raped, and terrorized in prison. Her crime? Being a member of the opposition party. "When they torture you, two things happen," she says. "First they make you crazy. Next, you believe you're going to so there's no point in confessing."

"I Never Revealed Anything"

Given the harshness of the interrogation techniques his administration authorized, former President George W. Bush was disingenuous when he insisted in 2006 that the US doesn't torture. He should first have consulted his father, a former CIA director, about the effectiveness of torturing an enemy.

> **FAST FACT**
>
> A 2009 CBS News/*New York Times* poll found that the majority of Americans—46 percent—said it is never justified to use waterboarding and other aggressive interrogation tactics to get information from a suspected terrorist. Thirty seven percent said it is sometimes justified, 7 percent said "it depends," and 10 percent were unsure.

An Ethiopian named Thomas spoke to that. "Instead of breaking you, it [torture] hardens you," he says. Security forces threatened to shoot him, saying, "We're just going to kill you. No one can save you. We'll say we shot you trying to escape."

"You think you are losing your mind," he recalls. But, the former nongovernmental organization worker adds proudly, "I never revealed anything."

It was the same with Miguel. Drunken soldiers walked him to a beach, pointing guns at him and asking, "You want us to bury you here six feet deep or out there 10 feet underwater?" He collapsed in a faint.

The Fallacy of Torture

The waterboarding technique used by American interrogators this past decade is little different: It's an implicit threat to kill suspects through drowning—Russian roulette played with a wet towel. To see for yourself, watch journalist Christopher Hitchens (voluntarily) get waterboarded on YouTube. Last year, President [Barack] Obama banned waterboarding.

Members of the group Torture Abolition and Survivors Support Coalition protest against alleged abuses at Guantánamo Bay prison.

Fortunate torture survivors sometimes get asylum in the US. By word of mouth, they learn of TASSC. Officials Miguel and Daoud, both torture survivors, shepherd the newcomers, finding them psychiatric help and shelter. In group counseling, perhaps the most difficult question they deal with is, "Why did this happen to me?"

A 2006 survey showed that a third of the world supports some degree of torture to combat terrorism. Yet we deceive ourselves pretending it does not also destroy our own decency and humanity. Support for torture was highest in Israel, at 43 percent; it was 36 percent in America. The fallacy of torture is the notion that terrorizing others makes us more secure.

EVALUATING THE AUTHOR'S ARGUMENTS:

To make his argument that torture is never justified, Rodgers quotes from people who have experienced torture. In your opinion, what did these first-person testimonials lend to his argument? Did it make you more likely to sympathize with people who have been tortured? Or did including such testimonials not convince you to agree with Rodgers that torture is never justified? Explain your reasoning.

The Use of Torture Can Save American Lives

Gary Bauer

"You do what you have to do to save those innocent lives, which in this case means waterboarding the terrorist. You are saving other people's families."

Torture is justified if it saves innocent lives, argues Gary Bauer in the following viewpoint. Bauer discusses Just War Theory, which lays out the criteria by which Christians have justified engaging in conflict for centuries. Bauer says that if torture meets all the criteria of a just war, then its use should be permitted. He believes that when it comes to terrorism, torture often does meet this criteria—it is used to prevent behavior that would be lasting, grave, and certain, and it often succeeds where other techniques fail. But most importantly, argues Bauer, the use of torture can save innocent lives. In his mind, there is no more justifiable cause than this. Bauer says that the use of torture has already saved people from dozens of terrorist attacks in both the United States and other nations. He concludes that torture prevents the death of innocent people and thus can be viewed as a form of self-defense.

Gary Bauer, "Just War Theory and Enhanced Interrogation: How Christians Can Think About the Unthinkable." This article originally appeared in *Townhall* magazine, and is reprinted by permission of the author.

Bauer is the president of American Values, a conservative organization opposed to such social issues as gay marriage, abortion, and the proposed Islamic Cultural Center at Ground Zero.

AS YOU READ, CONSIDER THE FOLLOWING QUESTIONS:
1. Who is Eleno Oviedo, and why does Bauer think he is different from someone like terrorist Khalid Sheikh Mohammed?
2. When was a Christian version of Just War Theory first posited, and by whom?
3. Where does Bauer say officials have used torture to successfully prevent terrorist attacks? Name two places.

A Thought Experiment: You walk into your home to find an armed intruder threatening to shoot your spouse and children, trapped with nowhere to run. Fortunately, you have a gun.

You try to negotiate, but the intruder is in no mood to talk. His intention is murder.

You have seconds to decide. What do you do?

For many, the answer is clear. You fight to save your family. And most of us would call that self defense. Most Christians would agree that any action would be not only morally permissible, but also morally required.

Now imagine another scenario: You are a CIA interrogator facing an avowed terrorist who was caught in the act of preparing for murder. You know he has information about a plot to blow up an unidentified building in a large American city. Innocent lives hang in the balance.

For hours you have attempted to extract the life-saving information from him, but to no avail. The last option is one you believe will work: water-boarding, but you have only a few minutes to decide. What do you do?

Again, for most of us, the answer is clear. You do what you have to do to save those innocent lives, which in this case means water-boarding the terrorist. You are saving other people's families.

Intent Makes All the Difference

In the continuing debate over the morality of enhanced interrogation, an essential consideration is often overlooked: intent. For Christians, intent is integral to determining whether and when certain techniques, including water-boarding, are morally permissible.

Historically, various forms of harsh interrogation have been employed as a means to punish, humiliate, intimidate, exact revenge or force a confession. Consider Cuba, where for half a century torture has been used to punish, humiliate and intimidate those who speak

Saint Augustine (354–430) first applied biblical principles to make judgments about the issues of war and torture.

out against the ruling Marxist [after the philosophy of Karl Marx] regime and for democratic values and basic human rights.

In an interview for this piece, Cuban Eleno Oviedo recalled the torture he experienced as a political prisoner of 26 years in [Cuban leader Fidel] Castro's prisons. "I was stripped in a cell and left in solitary confinement for the first 126 days," he said about the time after his initial abduction. The regime's intention, Oviedo said, was to get him to confess to being a CIA agent. Oviedo, who now lives in the United States, said that other political prisoners were left naked for weeks at a time. Some prisoners' fingers were cut or had their fingernails torn off. Others received beatings so severe that they died. And "three-hundred times I heard prisoners being executed" by firing squad, Oviedo recalled. And the torture continues. The horrors of Castro's gulag make us recoil in disgust, and their intentions and methods of torture should be rejected by a just society.

However, the issue which has been ignored to date in the discussion of enhanced interrogation is whether there is a difference between inflicting pain for its own sake or using some harsher methods with deliberation when lives are on the line. When the intent is to extract information necessary to save human beings in imminent danger, harsh treatment may be justified and, I believe, sometimes necessary.

War and Its Tools Have Long Been Justified

Just War Theory offers criteria for Christians to consider when determining under what circumstances enhanced interrogations may be justified. With roots in Greek and Roman philosophy, Just War Theory was given a Christian formulation in the Fourth Century when St. Augustine applied biblical principles to this very human question: When is war justified?

Most Americans Believe Harsh Interrogation Techniques Keep the Country Safe

A 2009 poll of registered voters found that the majority think using harsh interrogation techniques on captured and suspected terrorists keeps them safe by preventing and thwarting terrorist plots.

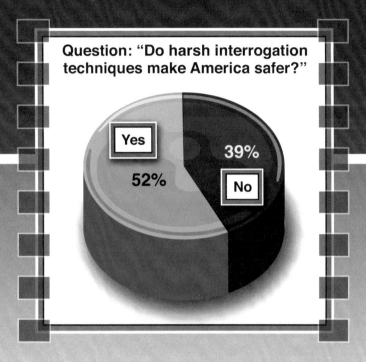

Question: "Do harsh interrogation techniques make America safer?"

Yes 52%

No 39%

Taken from: AM&A, Resurgent Republic National Survey of Registered Voters, May 11–14, 2009.

The Christian Just War Doctrine derives from a need to reconcile various Bible passages. Jesus tells us to "turn the other cheek", but he also told the apostles "let him who has no sword sell his mantel and buy one". Also, in the Old Testament's book of Ecclesiastes we are told that there is "a time to kill."

Under Just War Theory, a war is just only if it is defensive and meets four strict conditions. The requirements are: that the damage inflicted by the aggressor must be lasting, grave and certain; that there must be serious prospects of success; that all other means of ending the war must be shown to be impractical or ineffective; and that the use of force cannot produce evils graver than those to be eliminated.

Applying the first of the criterion to the water-boarding debate, we can better analyze the proverbial ticking time-bomb scenario. It is an extreme example, but it is not as rare as some suggest. Israeli authorities say they have thwarted dozens of imminent terrorist attacks saving countless civilian lives. These successes with water-boarding and other enhanced interrogation also help fulfill the second requirement of just war, that there must be serious prospects of success. The CIA's water-boarding of al Qaeda leader Khalid Sheik Mohammed (KSM) compelled him to reveal information that allowed the U.S. government to thwart a planned attack on Los Angeles. CIA officials have stated that they would not have been able to obtain critical information to prevent attacks without the use of enhanced interrogation including water-boarding. They had tried other means and failed.

Reports recently released by the Justice Department state that information elicited from KSM "dramatically expanded our universe of knowledge of Al Qaeda's plots." Former CIA director George Tenet has said, "From our interrogation of KSM and other senior al Qaeda members . . . we learned many things. For example, more than 20 plots had been put in motion by al Qaeda against U.S. infrastructure targets, including communications nodes, nuclear power plants, dams, bridges and tunnels."

The third criterion is that all other means of ending the war must be impractical or ineffective. CIA memos revealed that less harsh interrogation was always used before water-boarding was employed. Methods used included stress positions, loud music and confinement in small spaces, but those tools were not enough.

The fourth criterion might be the most difficult to meet. It is that the use of force cannot produce evils greater than those to be eliminated. In the case of Mohammad, innocent lives were saved as a consequence of the information received by interrogation officials after water-boarding, which, as agonizing as it can be, leaves no long-term physical effects on the prisoners. In fact, some of our own soldiers are water-boarded as part of their training.

Saving Innocent Lives Is Always Justified

It is vital in times like these to have a vigorous debate about how best to defend our nation. Christians especially are troubled by the reality that "the heart is deceitfully wicked, and who can know it?" We need to let the light of public debate shine into the darkness of the dangers we are confronting and of the temptations in the hearts of men and women to go too far against an enemy committed to our destruction.

Enhanced interrogation is not to be considered lightly, but the use of enhanced interrogation techniques does not require moral people to abandon their beliefs. Rather, it is precisely during these difficult times that one's beliefs about life, justice and mercy become indispensible. Just War Theory applied to the thorny issue of torture acknowledges the dignity of all human life and the abhorrence of torture. But it also creates a set of conditions that, if met, justify the use of force to save innocent lives facing imminent death.

> **EVALUATING THE AUTHOR'S ARGUMENTS:**
>
> Bauer claims that waterboarding does not cause any long-term trauma in people who experience it. How do you think the other authors in this chapter would respond to this claim? Write one to two sentences per author. Then, state your opinion of whether you think torture leaves a long-lasting effect on its victims and why you feel this way.

The Use of Torture Puts American Lives at Risk

Matthew Alexander

> "Our policy of torture and abuse of prisoners has been Al Qaida's number one recruiting tool."

Torturing captured terrorists puts American lives at risk, argues Matthew Alexander in the following viewpoint. Alexander says that America's use of torture has inspired many terrorists and would-be terrorists to attack American soldiers abroad. In fact, Alexander estimates that the use of torture by the United States is responsible for hundreds, and possibly thousands, of troop deaths. In addition, tortured terrorists are less likely to cooperate during interrogations and are less likely to negotiate with their captors. Alexander says that treating terrorist captives harshly undermines counterterrorism efforts and threatens the lives of American civilians and soldiers. He concludes there are smarter and less harsh ways to deal with America's enemies. Alexander is a fourteen-year veteran of the US Air Force. He served as the leader of an elite interrogations team in Iraq. In this role he conducted more than three hundred interrogations. "Matthew Alexander" is a pseudonym the author writes under to protect his identity.

Matthew Alexander, "Torture Doesn't Work," *The Daily Beast*. www.thedailybeast.com. Copyright © 2009 RTST, LLC. Reprinted by permission.

AS YOU READ, CONSIDER THE FOLLOWING QUESTIONS:
1. What does the author say is the main reason foreign fighters were motivated to go to Iraq and fight American forces?
2. What, according to Alexander, makes captured al Qaeda members willing to negotiate and cooperate with American forces?
3. Who are Khalid Sheikh Muhammad and Abu Zubaydah and how do they factor into the author's argument?

There are valid reasons why we haven't had enough with "torture sanctimony," as Christopher Buckley puts it in an article in *The Daily Beast,* and let me start with the most important—it's going to cost us future American lives in addition to the ones we've already lost.

Our policy of torture and abuse of prisoners has been Al Qaida's number one recruiting tool, a point that Buckley does not mention and is also conspicuously absent from former CIA Director General Michael Hayden and former Attorney General Michael Mukasey's argument

Graffiti images of the inmates who were tortured by US soldiers at the Abu Ghraib prison appear on walls in Iraq.

Interrogation Techniques Observed in Guantánamo

An extensive Department of Justice report polled FBI agents about how often they saw the following interrogation tactics in use at Guantánamo Bay detention facility in Cuba. Sexual humiliation, shackles, stress positions, and sleep deprivation were among the tactics witnessed.

Interrogation Technique	Personally Observed	Observed/Led Me to Believe	Detainee Told Me	Others Described to Me	None of the Above
Depriving a detainee of food or water	1	1	4	3	433
Depriving a detainee of clothing	3	1	4	5	433
Depriving a detainee of sleep, or interrupting sleep by frequent cell relocations or other methods	13	10	17	54	354
Beating a detainee			11	1	430
Using water to prevent breathing by a detainee or to create the sensation of drowning				1	441
Threatening other action to cause physical pain, injury, disfigurement, or death	2		1	4	435
Using shackles or other restraints in a prolonged manner	15	2	1	8	420
Requiring a detainee to maintain, or restraining a detainee in, a stressful or painful position	9	1	3	12	421
Intentionally delaying or denying detainee medical care			3	1	442
Hooding or blindfolding a detainee other than during transportation	9		1	2	431
Subjecting a detainee to extremely cold or hot room temperatures for extended periods	3	2	6	15	420
Subjecting a detainee to loud music	27		6	27	384
Subjecting a detainee to bright flashing lights or darkness	19		2	19	403

Interrogation Technique	Personally Observed	Observed/Led Me to Believe	Detainee Told Me	Others Described to Me	None of the Above
Isolating a detainee for an extended period	30	5	1	22	384
Using duct tape to restrain, gag, or punish a detainee	2			4	438
Using rapid response teams and/or forced cell extractions	11	8	9	43	376
Using a military working dog on or near a detainee other than during detainee transportation	3			6	434
Disrespectful statements, handling, or actions involving the Koran	2		19	10	414
Shaving a detainee's facial or other hair to embarrass or humiliate a detainee	3	4	6	6	427
Placing a woman's clothing on a detainee			2	4	441
Touching a detainee or acting toward a detainee in a sexual manner	2	2	2	11	426
Holding detainee(s) who is not officially acknowledged or registered as such by the agency detaining the person	2	1		1	438
Sending a detainee to another country for detention or more aggressive interrogation	1		2	2	434
Threatening to send a detainee to another country for detention or more aggressive interrogation	6		1	5	433
Threatening to take action against a detainee's family	2			2	439

Taken from: *A Review of the FBI's Involvement in and Observations of Detainee Interrogations in Guantanamo Bay, Afghanistan, and Iraq*, US Department of Justice, May 2008, pp. 172–173.

in the *Wall Street Journal*. As the senior interrogator in Iraq for a task force charged with hunting down Abu Musab Al Zarqawi, the former Al Qaida leader and mass murderer, I listened time and time again to captured foreign fighters cite the torture and abuse at Abu Ghraib and Guantanamo as their main reason for coming to Iraq to fight. Consider that 90 percent of the suicide bombers in Iraq are these foreign fighters and you can easily conclude that we have lost hundreds, if not thousands, of American lives because of our policy of torture and abuse. But that's only the *past*.

Somewhere in the world there are other young Muslims who have joined Al Qaida because we tortured and abused prisoners. These men will certainly carry out future attacks against Americans, either in Iraq, Afghanistan, or possibly even here. And that's not to mention numerous other Muslims who support Al Qaida, either financially or in other ways, because they are outraged that the United States tortured and abused Muslim prisoners.

In addition, torture and abuse has made us less safe because detainees are less likely to cooperate during interrogations if they don't trust us. I know from having conducted hundreds of interrogations of high ranking Al Qaida members and supervising more than one thousand, that when a captured Al Qaida member sees us live up to our stated principles they are more willing to negotiate and cooperate with us. When we torture or abuse them, it hardens their resolve and reaffirms why they picked up arms.

Former officials who say that we prevented terrorist attacks by waterboarding Khalid Sheikh Muhammad or Abu Zubaydah are possibly intentionally ignorant of the fact that their actions cost us American lives. And let's not forget the glaring failure in these cases. Torture never convinced either of these men to sell out Osama Bin Laden. And that's the other lesson I learned in Iraq.

Coercion convinces a detainee to give you the minimum (and often an altered minimum) amount of information. Note that KSM only provided information that was downward from him in the Al Qaida hierarchy. I saw the same results in Iraq. When other interrogators used fear and control to force detainees to provide information, that information, at best, was always downward or lateral in direction. Why? Because a detainee knows that they can sell out the people below them or even future operations and the organization will survive. It's been over seven years since 9/11 and we have yet to bring Osama Bin Laden to justice. He continues to recruit new terrorists, especially with our past policy of torture and abuse as a recruiting tool. So when I look at the squandered opportunity to locate him through KSM or Abu Zubaydah, I see failure.

Contrast that with my interrogation team in Iraq. We used relationship-building approaches, leveraged the best of our American culture (tolerance, cultural understanding, and intellect), and we ultimately found the head of Al Qaida in Iraq by being smarter, not harsher. We captured Al Qaida terrorists, some very high-ranking leaders, who never provided information. But we didn't resort to torture or abuse because we knew that it would have made us hypocrites to sell out the very principles that we were defending. We also knew that it would cost us the lives of our brothers and sisters in arms, our fellow soldiers. Instead, we used those as opportunities to become better interrogators and then concentrated on other avenues to achieve our mission. We can lose a battle and still win a war.

My extensive experience demonstrates that we can effectively interrogate without using torture and abuse. We do not have to choose between terror and torture. We are Americans and we are smarter and better than that.

EVALUATING THE AUTHOR'S ARGUMENTS:

The author of this viewpoint is a former soldier who has had experience interrogating captured terrorists. Does knowing his background make you more likely to agree with his argument? If so, why? If not, why not? Explain your reasoning.

Viewpoint
5

Torture Produces Reliable Information

Marc A. Thiessen

"Without enhanced interrogations, there could be a hole in the ground in Los Angeles to match the one in New York."

In the following viewpoint, Marc A. Thiessen explains that information provided by suspected terrorists has been used to successfully prevent further terrorist attacks. He argues, therefore, that using enhanced interrogation techniques extracts reliable information from terrorists. He discusses the case of several terrorists who provided reliable information after being interrogated in such a manner. According to Thiessen, this information turned out to be more than just credible—it was key to preventing several terrorist attacks that would have claimed the lives of thousands of Americans. Thiessen believes that terrorist suspects will talk if pressured in the right way. For this reason, he concludes, the United States should continue to use enhanced interrogation techniques on captured terrorists to protect Americans from further attacks. Thiessen served in senior positions in the Pentagon and the White House from 2001 to 2009.

Marc A. Thiessen, "Enhanced Interrogations Worked," *Washington Post,* April 21, 2009. Reprinted by permission of the author.

He was also a chief speechwriter for former president George W. Bush. He is currently a visiting fellow at the Hoover Institution.

AS YOU READ, CONSIDER THE FOLLOWING QUESTIONS:
1. What, according to a May 30, 2005, Justice Department memo, was key to preventing an al Qaeda attack in the West?
2. What information does the author say suspected terrorist Abu Zubaydah provided to officials after he was subjected to controversial interrogation tactics?
3. What does Thiessen say Islamic terrorists are called by their faith to do? Which piece of his argument does this information support?

I n releasing highly classified documents on the CIA interrogation program last week [in April 2009], President [Barack] Obama declared that the techniques used to question captured terrorists "did not make us safer." This is patently false. The proof is in the memos Obama made public—in sections that have gone virtually unreported in the media.

Harsh Interrogation Tactics Worked

Consider the Justice Department memo of May 30, 2005. It notes that

> the CIA believes "the intelligence acquired from these interrogations has been a key reason why al Qaeda has failed to launch a spectacular attack in the West since 11 September 2001.". . . In particular, the CIA believes that it would have been unable to obtain critical information from numerous detainees, including [9/11 mastermind] [Khalid Sheik Mohammed] and [war on terror detainee] Abu Zubaydah, without these enhanced techniques.

The memo continues: "Before the CIA used enhanced techniques . . . KSM [Mohammed] resisted giving any answers to questions about future attacks, simply noting, 'Soon you will find out.'" Once the techniques were applied, "interrogations have led to specific, actionable intelligence, as well as a general increase in the amount of intelligence regarding al Qaeda and its affiliates."

Specifically, interrogation with enhanced techniques "led to the discovery of a KSM plot, the 'Second Wave,' to use East Asian operatives to crash a hijacked airliner into' a building in Los Angeles." KSM later acknowledged before a military commission at Guantanamo Bay that the target was the Library Tower, the tallest building on the West Coast. The memo explains that "information obtained from KSM also led to the capture of Riduan bin Isomuddin, better known as Hambali, and the discovery of the Guraba Cell, a 17-member Jemmah Islamiyah cell tasked with executing the 'Second Wave.'" In other words, without enhanced interrogations, there could be a hole in the ground in Los Angeles to match the one in New York.

Information Extracted from Terrorists Has Proved Useful

The memo notes that "[i]nterrogations of [Abu] Zubaydah—again, enhanced techniques were employed—furnished detailed information regarding al Qaeda's 'organizational structure, key operatives,

FAST FACT

The "ticking time bomb" scenario—which suggests that torture can be justified if it can successfully get information out of a terrorist who has details of an imminent attack—was first posited by the French author Jean Lartéguy in the 1960 novel *Les Centurions*.

and modus operandi' and identified KSM as the mastermind of the September 11 attacks." This information helped the intelligence community plan the operation that captured KSM. It went on: "Zubaydah and KSM also supplied important information about [Abu Musab] al-Zarqawi and his network" in Iraq, which helped our operations against al-Qaeda in that country.

All this confirms information that I and others have described publicly. But just as the memo begins to describe previously undisclosed details of what enhanced interrogations achieved, the page is almost entirely blacked out. The Obama administration released pages of unredacted classified information on the techniques used to question captured terrorist leaders

Terrorist detainee Abu Zubaydah provided important information about al Qaeda and Abu Musab al-Zarqawi after being subjected to "enhanced interrogation techniques."

but pulled out its black marker when it came to the details of what those interrogations achieved.

Yet there is more information confirming the program's effectiveness. The Office of Legal Counsel memo states "we discuss only a small fraction of the important intelligence CIA interrogators have obtained from KSM" and notes that "intelligence derived from CIA detainees has resulted in more than 6,000 intelligence reports and, in 2004, accounted for approximately half of the [Counterterrorism

Center's] reporting on al Qaeda." The memos refer to other classified documents—including an "Effectiveness Memo" and an "IG Report," which explain how "the use of enhanced techniques in the interrogations of KSM, Zubaydah and others . . . has yielded critical information." Why didn't Obama officials release this information as well? Because they know that if the public could see the details of the techniques side by side with evidence that the program saved American lives, the vast majority would support continuing it.

Critics claim that enhanced techniques do not produce good intelligence because people will say anything to get the techniques to stop. But the memos note that, "as Abu Zubaydah himself explained with respect to enhanced techniques, 'brothers who are captured and interrogated are permitted by Allah to provide information when they believe they have reached the limit of their ability to withhold it in the face of psychological and physical hardship.'" In other words, the terrorists are called by their faith to resist as far as they can—and once they have done so, they are free to tell everything they know. This is because of their belief that "Islam will ultimately dominate the world and that this victory is inevitable." The job of the interrogator is to safely help the terrorist do his duty to Allah, so he then feels liberated to speak freely.

Do Not Change US Policy Now

This is the secret to the program's success. And the [Barack] Obama administration's decision to share this secret with the terrorists threatens our national security. Al-Qaeda will use this information and other details in the memos to train its operatives to resist questioning and withhold information on planned attacks. CIA Director Leon Panetta said during his confirmation hearings that even the Obama administration might use some of the enhanced techniques in a "ticking time bomb" scenario. What will the administration do now that it has shared the limits of our interrogation techniques with the enemy? President Obama's decision to release these documents is one of the most dangerous and irresponsible acts ever by an American president during a time of war—and Americans may die as a result.

EVALUATING THE AUTHOR'S ARGUMENTS:

Marc A. Thiessen quotes from several sources to support the points he makes in his essay. Make a list of everyone he quotes, including their credentials and the nature of their comments. Then, analyze his sources: Are they credible? Are they well qualified to speak on this subject? What specific points do they support?

Viewpoint 6

Torture Results in Unreliable Information

David Rose

> *"Not only have coercive methods failed to generate significant and actionable intelligence, they have also caused the squandering of resources on a massive scale."*

Information divulged under torture is notoriously unreliable and worthless, argues David Rose in the following viewpoint. Rose explains that people who are tortured are likely to lie or invent details just to make the torture stop. Therefore, information extracted from a subject under such circumstances is likely to be suspect, tainted, or otherwise wrong and unreliable. Rose argues that such tainted information has led the United States astray in the past, most recently preceding the 2003 invasion of Iraq. He claims that officials used information obtained under torture to connect the terrorist organization al Qaeda to Iraq—information that later proved false. For this reason, concludes Rose, even senior counterterrorism officials recommend that torture not be used on captured and suspected terrorists.

Rose is a contributing editor for *Vanity Fair*, where this viewpoint was originally published.

David Rose, "Tortured Reasoning," *Vanity Fair*, December 16, 2008. Reprinted by permission of the author.

AS YOU READ, CONSIDER THE FOLLOWING QUESTIONS:
  1. Who is Friedrich von Spee and how does he factor into the author's argument?
  2. What kinds of information does Rose say Egyptian terrorist Mahmud Abouhalima divulged after being tortured?
  3. In what way was faulty intelligence used to justify the US invasion of Iraq, according to Rose?

Abu Zubaydah [was] the first U.S. prisoner in the Global War on Terror to undergo waterboarding.

The case of [al Qaeda lieutenant] Abu Zubaydah is a suitable place to begin answering some pressing but little-considered questions. Putting aside all legal and ethical issues (not to mention the P.R. ramifications), does such treatment—categorized unhesitatingly by the International Committee of the Red Cross as torture—actually work, in the sense of providing reliable, actionable intelligence? Is it superior to other interrogation methods, and if they had the choice, free of moral qualms or the fear of prosecution, would interrogators use it freely? . . .

Torture Fails to Generate High-Quality Intelligence

In researching this article, I spoke to numerous counterterrorist officials from agencies on both sides of the Atlantic. Their conclusion is unanimous: not only have coercive methods failed to generate significant and actionable intelligence, they have also caused the squandering of resources on a massive scale through false leads, chimerical [improbable] plots, and unnecessary safety alerts—with Abu Zubaydah's case one of the most glaring examples.

Here, they say, far from exposing a deadly plot, all torture did was lead to more torture of his supposed accomplices while also providing some misleading "information" that boosted the administration's argument for invading Iraq. . . .

Torture Begets Lies and Worthless Statements

There is, alas, no shortage of evidence from earlier times that torture produces bad intelligence. "It is incredible what people say under the compulsion of torture," wrote the German Jesuit Friedrich von Spee in 1631, "and how many lies they will tell about themselves and about others; in the end, whatever the torturers want to be true, is true."

The unreliability of intelligence acquired by torture was taken as a given in the early years of the C.I.A., whose 1963 kubark interrogation manual stated: "Intense pain is quite likely to produce false confessions, concocted as a means of escaping from distress. A time-consuming delay results, while investigation is conducted and the admissions are proven untrue. During this respite the interrogatee can pull himself together. He may even use the time to think up new, more complex 'admissions' that take still longer to disprove."

A 1957 study by Albert Biderman, an Air Force sociologist, described how brainwashing had been achieved by depriving prisoners of sleep, exposing them to cold, and forcing them into agonizing "stress positions" for long periods. In July 2008, *The New York Times* reported that Biderman's work formed the basis of a 2002 interrogators' training class at Guantánamo Bay. That the methods it described had once been used to generate Communist propaganda had apparently been forgotten.

Experience derived from 1990s terrorism cases also casts doubt on torture's value. For example, in March 1993, F.B.I. agents flew to Cairo to take charge of an Egyptian named Mahmud Abouhalima, who would be convicted for having bombed the World Trade Center a month earlier. Abouhalima had already been tortured by Egyptian intelligence agents for 10 days, and had the wounds to prove it. As U.S. investigators should have swiftly realized, his statements in Egypt were worthless, among them claims that the bombing was sponsored by Iranian businessmen, although, apparently, their sworn enemy, Iraq, had also played a part. . . .

Unreliable Information

On March 27, 2007, Abu Zubaydah was able to make a rare public statement, at a "Combatant Status-Review Tribunal" at Guantánamo—a military hearing convened to determine whether he should continue to be detained. Everything he said about the details of his treatment was redacted from the unclassified record. But a few relevant remarks remain:

I was nearly before half die plus [because] what they do [to] torture me. There I was not afraid from die because I do believe I will be shahid [martyr], but as God make me as a human and I weak, so they say yes, I say okay, I do I do, but leave me. They say no, we don't want to. You to admit you do this, we want you to give us more information . . . they want what's after more information about more operations, so I can't. They keep torturing me.

Justice Department Inspector General Glenn Fine testified before the US Senate Judiciary Committee that the CIA's advanced interrogation techniques would "not be effective in obtaining accurate information."

The tribunal president, a colonel whose name is redacted, asked him: "So I understand that during this treatment, you said things to make them stop and then those statements were actually untrue, is that correct?" Abu Zubaydah replied: "Yes."

FAST FACT

The *Los Angeles Times* reported in 2009 that Khalid Sheikh Mohammed, mastermind of the September 11, 2001, terrorist attacks, lied to CIA officials after being abused.

Some of those statements, say two senior intelligence analysts who worked on them at the time, concerned the issue that in the spring of 2002 interested the [George W.] Bush administration more than almost any other—the supposed operational relationship between al-Qaeda and Iraq. Given his true position in the jihadist hierarchy, Abu Zubaydah "would not have known that if it was true," says [FBI counterterrorist expert Dan] Coleman. "But you can lead people down a course and make them say anything."

Some of what he did say was leaked by the administration: for example, the claim that [Osama] bin Laden and his ally Abu Musab al-Zarqawi were working directly with [former Iraqi president] Saddam Hussein to destabilize the autonomous Kurdish region in northern Iraq. There was much more, says the analyst who worked at the Pentagon: "I first saw the reports soon after Abu Zubaydah's capture. There was a lot of stuff about the nuts and bolts of al-Qaeda's supposed relationship with the Iraqi Intelligence Service. The intelligence community was lapping this up, and so was the administration, obviously. Abu Zubaydah was saying Iraq and al-Qaeda had an operational relationship. It was everything the administration hoped it would be."

Information Obtained Under Torture Is Tainted

Within the administration, Abu Zubaydah's interrogation was "an important chapter," the second analyst says: overall, his interrogation "product" was deemed to be more significant than the claims made by Ibn al-Shaykh al-Libi, another al-Qaeda captive, who in early 2002 was tortured in Egypt at the C.I.A.'s behest. After all, Abu Zubaydah was being interviewed by Americans. Like the former Pentagon official, this official had no idea that Abu Zubaydah had been tortured.

"As soon as I learned that the reports had come from torture, once my anger had subsided I understood the damage it had done," the Pentagon analyst says. "I was so angry, knowing that the higher-ups in the administration knew he was tortured, and that the information he was giving up was tainted by the torture, and that it became one reason to attack Iraq."

One result of Abu Zubaydah's torture was that the F.B.I.'s assistant director for counterterrorism, Pasquale D'Amuro, persuaded Director Robert Mueller that the bureau should play no part in future C.I.A. interrogations that used extreme techniques forbidden by the F.B.I. The Justice Department's Glenn Fine indicated in a statement before the U.S. Senate that the main reason was that the agency's techniques would "not be effective in obtaining accurate information."

EVALUATING THE AUTHORS' ARGUMENTS:

David Rose and Marc A. Thiessen (author of the previous viewpoint) disagree over whether information extracted from terrorists via torture is reliable. In your opinion, which author made the better argument? Why? List at least four pieces of evidence (quotes, statistics, facts, or statements of reasoning) that caused you to side with one author over the other.

Torture Violates American Values

Eric Margolis

In the following viewpoint, Eric Margolis argues that torture is inherently un-American. In his opinion, any nation that employs torture disgraces itself and earns a dangerous reputation for revolting, shameful behavior. He points out that America's use of torture gives it something in common with some of its worst enemies, such as the Japanese during World War II, the leaders of the former Soviet Union, and the current North Korean government. In his opinion, torture results in inaccurate information and puts both soldiers and civilians at risk. Margolis suggests that America right its reputation by putting American officials who condone torture on trial for war crimes.

Margolis is a contributing foreign editor for Sun National Media Canada. He is also the author of *American Raj: Liberation or Domination? Resolving the Conflict Between the West and the Muslim World.*

"Torture is a crime under US law. . . . Torture violates core American values."

Eric Margolis, "America's Shame," LewRockwell.com, April 28, 2009. Reprinted by permission.

AS YOU READ, CONSIDER THE FOLLOWING QUESTIONS:
1. What two anti-torture treaties has the United States signed, according to the author?
2. For what crime did the United States hang Japanese officers after World War II, according to Margolis? What part of his argument does this support?
3. What does the author say CIA and US military interrogators learned from the North Koreans and the Soviets?

Nations that use torture disgrace themselves. Armed forces and police that torture inevitably become brutalized and corrupted. "Limited" use of torture quickly becomes generalized. "Information" obtained by torture is mostly unreliable.

I learned these truths over fifty years covering dirty "pacification" wars, from Algeria to Indochina, Central and South America, southern Africa, the Mideast, Afghanistan, and Kashmir in which torture was commonly used.

Revolting and Shameful

In spite of all the historical evidence that torture is counterproductive, the [George W.] Bush administration encouraged torture of anti-American militants (aka "terrorists") after the 9/11 attacks. The full story has not yet been revealed, but what we know so far is revolting and shameful. Britain and Canada were also complicit as they used information derived from torture and handed suspects over to be tortured.

Many Americans and human rights groups are now demanding that the Bush administration officials who employed and sanctioned torture face justice. President Barack Obama hinted his new attorney general, Eric Holder, might investigate this whole ugly business. But the Obama White House clearly wants to dodge this issue.

Republicans, who have become America's champion of war and torture, are fiercely resisting any investigation, and lauding torture's benefits. Just when it seemed impossible for the dumbed-down Republican redneck party to sink any lower, it has by endorsing torture as the American way.

FBI director Robert Mueller told the US Senate that torture techniques had not prevented any attacks against the United States.

So, too, some senior intelligence and Pentagon officials including, dismayingly, Obama's new CIA chief, Leon Panetta. He should know better. Many senior Congressional Democrats who sanctioned torture, or did nothing to stop it, are equally reluctant that the torture scandal be further investigated.

Torture Violates Our Values—And Gets Us Nothing

Torture is a crime under US law. It is a crime under the Third Geneva Convention, and the UN's [United Nations'] Anti-Torture Convention, both of which the US signed. Kidnapping and moving suspects to be tortured in third countries is a crime. Torture violates core American values.

In 1945, the US hanged Japanese officers for inflicting "waterboarding" (near-drowning) on US prisoners, which were deemed war crimes. Yet this is exactly what the CIA inflicted on its Muslim captives. FBI agents rightly refused to participate in the torture of al-Qaeda suspects, warning that it violated US law and could make them subject to future prosecution.

Republicans and even Obama's intelligence chief, Adm. Dennis Blair, claim some useful information was obtained by torture. That depends on what you call useful. Al-Qaeda is still in business. Osama bin Laden remains at large. Iraq and Afghanistan became monstrous fiascoes costing $1 trillion. US military and intelligence personnel who fall into hostile hands may now face similar tortures.

In 2004, CIA's inspector general reported there was *no proof* that use of torture had thwarted "specific imminent attacks." This comes from a recently declassified Justice Department memo.

Torture Has Not Protected America

The director of the FBI, Robert Mueller, one of Washington's most upright, respected officials, also declared that torture had not prevented any attacks against the United States. Both findings directly contradict claims by . . . [former vice president] Dick Cheney, that torture prevented major attacks.

Torture did not protect America from a second major attack, as Republicans claim. In fact, it appears 9/11 was a one-off event, and al-Qaeda numbered only a handful of extremists to begin with, not the worldwide conspiracy claimed by the White House after it was caught sleeping on guard duty. Bush administration claims about imminent threats from dirty bombs and germ weapons such as anthrax were untrue.

CIA "useful" torture information came from two suspects: [9/11 mastermind] Khalid Sheik Mohammed was tortured by near drowning 183 times—six times *daily* for a month; and [al Qaeda lieutenant] Abu Zubaydah, 83 times in August, 2003.

Use a power drill (a favorite "investigative" tool of America's Iraqi Shia allies) on Dick Cheney, and it would take only minutes to get him to admit he's Osama bin Laden.

Adopting the Techniques of Our Enemies

A shocking US Senate report just revealed that after the Bush administration could not find the links it claimed existed between al-Qaeda and [former Iraqi leader] Saddam Hussein, it tried, in best Soviet style, to torture its captives to admit that such links did, in fact, exist. That, of course, would have been a much better excuse for invading Iraq than the lies about weapons of mass destruction pointed at America.

The Senate also reported CIA and Pentagon torture techniques were adopted from torture methods North Korea used in the 1950's to compel American prisoners to confess to lies about germ warfare.

FAST FACT

The US Supreme Court ruled in the 2006 case *Hamdan v. Rumsfeld* that certain treatment of the Guantánamo Bay detainees—such as trying them in special military commissions—would violate the Geneva Conventions' Common Article 3.

In fact, North Korea learned its torture techniques from Soviet KGB [secret police] instructors. KGB's favorite tortures in the 1930's and 40's were merciless beatings, confinement in refrigerated cells, week-long sleep deprivation, and endless interrogations. I have seen the torture cells at KGB's Lubiyanka HQ in Moscow.

The CIA and US military copied these North Korean/Soviet torture methods, but also added contorted positions, and nakedness and humiliation, techniques learned from Israeli interrogators who used them to blackmail Palestinian prisoners into becoming informers. Hence all the naked photos from Abu Ghraib prison.

Those Who Tortured Should Be Brought to Justice

American doctors and medical personnel supervised torture and devised and supervised techniques to mentally incapacitate prisoners through isolation, terrifying sensory deprivation, and injections of potent psychotropic drugs.

Torture was authorized by President George W. Bush, VP Dick Cheney, Secretaries Don Rumsfeld and Condoleezza Rice, and carried out by CIA chief George Tenet and the Pentagon's secretive Special Operations Command.

Four lickspittle lawyers and two bootlicking attorney generals provided sophistic legal briefs sanctioning torture. All should

THE DICK CHENEY REDESIGN

TORTURE OF OUR ENEMIES IS AN AMERICAN VALUE

steve@greenberg-art.com

GREENBERG

"Statue of Torture," cartoon by Steve Greenberg, *VCReporter*, September 3, 2009. www.PoliticalCartoons .com. Copyright © 2009 Steve Greenberg and CagleCartoons.com. All Rights Reserved.

be disbarred and face an independent judicial commission. Not a whitewash, like the 9/11 Commission, but a real, independent legal body. Better, send the case to the UN International Court in The Hague.

Americans Do Not Just "Follow Orders"

President Obama actually told CIA personnel that he does not want to prosecute the torturers because they were only following proper legal advice and orders. So did Nazi officials who killed millions.

Nazi lawyers legally dismembered Germany's Weimar democracy [the parliamentary republic established in 1919] and imposed Nazi dictatorship in only two months after the "terrorist attack" on the Reichstag in Feb. 1933.[1] Imposition of [Nazi leader Adolf] Hitler's dictatorship followed proper legal channels.

When I served in the US Army, I was taught that any illegal order, even from the president, must be refused and that mistreating prisoners was a crime.

1. The author is referring to the February 27, 1933, arson attack on the Reichstag, the German parliament. This was a key event in Adolf Hitler's rise to power and the establishment of the Nazi regime.

President Obama must show the world that America upholds the law, rejects torture of all kinds, and that no officials are above the law. Otherwise, there is no other way to prevent the recurrence of torture in the future.

EVALUATING THE AUTHOR'S ARGUMENTS:

Eric Margolis uses facts, statistics, examples, and reasoning to make his argument that torture is un-American. He does not, however, use any quotations to support his point. If you were to rewrite this article and insert quotations, what authorities might you quote from? Where would you place these quotes, and why?

Torture Does Not Violate American Values

Patrick J. Buchanan

"Is it ever moral to kill? Of course. We give guns to police and soldiers, and honor them as heroes when they use their guns to save lives."

In the following viewpoint Patrick J. Buchanan suggests that torture does not violate American values, if done to save American lives. He explains that although some Americans contend that the use of torture or enhanced interrogation techniques is evil, illegal, and demeaning, many others think the morality of these acts depends on what type of force is used and under what circumstances. Buchanan points out that there are many examples of moral use of typically immoral acts: Murder, for example, is typically immoral—yet society allows police and military to kill, and with good reason. Likewise, says Buchanan, inflicting pain is typically immoral, except for when doctors and surgeons use pain to heal or for another worthy purpose. In Buchanan's opinion, the use of torture to save American lives qualifies as such a worthy end.

Patrick J. Buchanan is a nationally syndicated columnist and author of *Churchill, Hitler, and "The Unnecessary War": How*

Patrick J. Buchanan, "Is Torture Ever Moral?," *Human Events*, April 28, 2009. Copyright © 2009 HUMAN EVENTS. All rights reserved. Reproduced by permission.

Britain Lost Its Empire and the West Lost the World, "The Death of the West," "The Great Betrayal," "A Republic, Not an Empire" and "Where the Right Went Wrong."

AS YOU READ, CONSIDER THE FOLLOWING QUESTIONS:
1. On what does the morality of killing or inflicting severe pain depend on, according to Buchanan?
2. According to the author, which snipers deserve death and which snipers deserve medals?
3. What is the plot of the movie *Taken* and how does it factor into Buchanan's argument?

After opening the door to a truth commission to investigate torture by the CIA of al-Qaida subjects, and leaving the door open to prosecution of higher-ups, President Obama walked the cat back.

He is now opposed to a truth commission. That means it is dead. He is no longer interested in prosecutions. That means no independent counsel—for now.

Sen. Harry Reid does not want any new "commissions, boards, tribunals, until we find out what the facts are." Thus, there will be none. The place to find out the facts, says the majority leader, is the intelligence committee of Sen. Dianne Feinstein.

Though belated, White House recognition that high-profile public hearings on the "enhanced interrogation techniques" used by the CIA in the Bush-Cheney years could divide the nation and rip this city apart is politically wise.

For any such investigation must move up the food chain from CIA interrogators, to White House lawyers, to the Cabinet officers who sit on the National Security Council, to Dick Cheney, to The Decider himself.

And what is the need to re-air America's dirty linen before a hostile world, when the facts are already known.

The CIA did use harsh treatment on al-Qaida. That treatment was sanctioned by White House and Justice Department lawyers.

The NSC, Cheney and President Bush did sign off. And Obama has ordered all such practices discontinued.

This is not a question of "What did the president know and when did he know it?" It is a question of the legality and morality of what is already known. And on this, the country is rancorously split.

Many contend that torture is inherently evil, morally outrageous and legally impermissible under both existing U.S. law and the Geneva Convention on prisoners of war.

Moreover, they argue, torture does not work.

Its harvest is hatred, deceptions and lies. And because it is cowardly and cruel, torture degrades those who do it, as well as those to whom it is done. It instills a spirit of revenge in its victims.

When the knowledge of torture is made public, as invariably it is, it besmirches America's good name and serves as a recruiting poster for our enemies and a justification to use the same degrading methods on our men and women.

And it makes us no better than the Chinese communist brainwashers of the Korean War, the Japanese war criminals who tortured U.S. POWs and the jailers at the Hanoi Hilton who tortured Sen. John McCain.

Moreover, even if done in a few monitored cases, where it seems to be the only way to get immediate intelligence to save hundreds

or thousands from imminent terror attack, down the chain of command they know it is being done. Thus, we get sadistic copycat conduct at Abu Ghraib by enlisted personnel to amuse themselves at midnight.

While the legal and moral case against torture is compelling, there is another side.

Let us put aside briefly the explosive and toxic term.

Is it ever moral to kill? Of course. We give guns to police and soldiers, and honor them as heroes when they use their guns to save lives.

The author of this viewpoint mentions that it is moral for police officers and soldiers to kill to save lives. Here US Air Force ground crew members inspect a F-15E Strike Eagle fighter jet before takeoff.

Is it ever moral to inflict excruciating pain? Of course. Civil War doctors who cut off arms and legs in battlefield hospitals saved many soldiers from death by gangrene.

The morality of killing or inflicting severe pain depends, then, not only on the nature of the act, but on the circumstances and motive.

The Beltway Snipers deserved death sentences. The Navy Seal snipers who killed those three Somali pirates and saved Captain Richard Phillips deserve medals.

Consider now Khalid Sheikh Mohammed, mastermind of 9-11, which sent 3,000 Americans to horrible deaths, and who was behind, if he did not do it himself, the beheading of Danny Pearl.

Even many opponents against torture will concede we have the same right to execute Khalid Mohammed as we did Timothy McVeigh. But if we have a right to kill him, do we have no moral right to waterboard him for 20 minutes to force him to reveal plans and al-Qaida accomplices to save thousands of American lives?

Americans are divided.

"Rendition," a film based on a true story, where an innocent man suspected of belonging to a terrorist cell is sent to an Arab country and tortured, won rave reviews.

But more popular was "Taken," a film in which Liam Neeson, an ex-spy, has a daughter kidnapped by white slavers in Paris, whom he tortures for information to rescue her and bring her home.

Certainly, Cheney and Bush, who make no apologies for what they authorized to keep America safe for seven and a half years, should be held to account. But so, too, should Barack Obama, if U.S. citizens die in a terror attack the CIA might have prevented, had its interrogators not been tied to an Army Field Manual written for dealing with soldiers, not al-Qaida killers who favor "soft targets" such as subways, airliners and office buildings.

EVALUATING THE AUTHOR'S ARGUMENTS:

In this viewpoint Patrick J. Buchanan suggests that if Americans have the right to sentence a convicted terrorist to the death penalty, they also have the right to waterboard him if it will produce information that will save innocent lives. What do you think? Do you think there is a connection between executing a terrorist and torturing him? Does one allow the other, or are they different scenarios entirely? Explain your reasoning.

Chapter 2

What Qualifies as Torture?

A sixteenth-century woodcut depicts a prisoner being tortured during the Spanish Inquisition.

Viewpoint

1

Enhanced Interrogation Techniques Are Torture

"It is torture when a prisoner is forced to stand while blood pools in his legs causing painful swelling and potentially life threatening blood clots."

Allen Keller

Allen Keller is the director of the Bellevue/ New York University Program for Survivors of Torture. In the following viewpoint he explains why he thinks enhanced interrogation techniques qualify as torture. These techniques—which include simulated drowning, forcing a prisoner to stay awake for weeks, and sexual humiliation—cause intense physical and mental suffering that can last a lifetime. In Keller's view, calling such tactics "enhanced interrogation" masks their true dehumanizing nature. He concludes that the American public should avoid using euphemisms for torture, and prosecute American officials who have allowed such tactics to be used.

AS YOU READ, CONSIDER THE FOLLOWING QUESTIONS:
1. What does Keller say detainees in the war on terror have in common with Tibetan monks and African students?
2. What is the SERE program and how does it factor into the author's argument?
3. What was the finding of a 2008 Physicians for Human Rights report, according to Keller?

Allen Keller, "Torture by Another Name," *HuffingtonPost.com,* 2009. Reprinted by permission of the author.

Misconceptions and distortions about torture by former Vice President [Dick] Cheney and other former [George W.] Bush administration officials are, if nothing else, impressive for their hubris. In a speech last Thursday [May 21, 2009], Mr. Cheney asserted that "tough" or "enhanced" interrogation methods were legal, essential, effective, and were not torture.

Mr. Cheney is wrong. Waterboarding, exposure to extremes of heat and cold, sexual humiliations and several other cruel and inhuman methods documented to have been used on known or suspected terrorists are forms of torture. My perspective is not theoretical. It is based on nearly 20 years of experience as a physician examining and caring for individuals from all over the world who endured torture and other cruel and inhuman treatment or punishment and studying the health consequences of such trauma. This includes Tibetan monks tortured because of their demands for independence, African students, tortured because of calling for democracy, and most recently, former detainees from Abu Ghraib[1] and Guantanamo [detention camp, a US facility based in Cuba].

One Can Only Call It Torture

Mr. Cheney derides the [Barack] Obama Administration for using "euphemisms that strive to put an imaginary distance between the American people and the terrorist enemy." He then goes on to repeatedly invoke the euphemism of "enhanced" interrogations instead of torture. This term infers a seemingly benign and improved means for eliciting information. It is neither.

It is torture when a prisoner is subjected to mock drowning—one of the most terrifying experiences conceivable. Water is poured over a detainee's face which is covered with a soaked cloth while his hands are tied causing him to gag and choke. It is torture when a prisoner is kept awake for weeks or longer by constant loud noises, bright lights or prison guards incessantly rattling the bars of his cell. It is torture when a prisoner is forced to stand while blood pools in his legs causing painful swelling and potentially life threatening blood clots. Forced nudity and sexual humiliations may seem more innocuous than being

1. An Iraqi prison where US soldiers abused Iraqi prisoners of war.

Yes, It Was Torture

A 2009 CNN poll revealed that the majority of Americans think that the harsh interrogation tactics authorized by the Bush administration qualified as torture. The majority of respondents supported their use regardless.

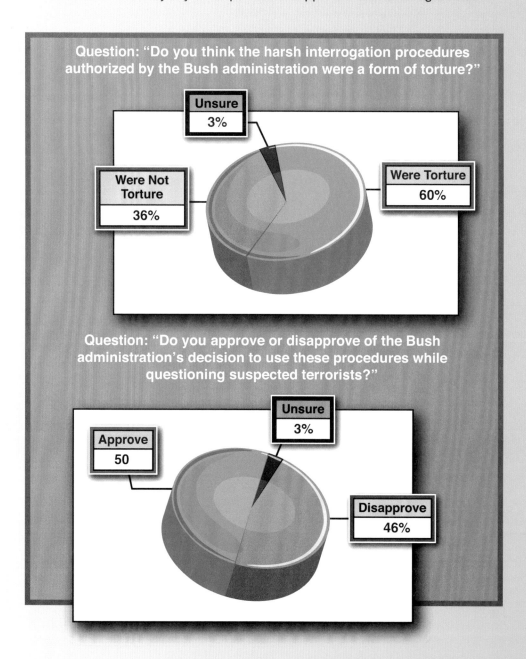

Question: "Do you think the harsh interrogation procedures authorized by the Bush administration were a form of torture?"

Unsure
3%

Were Not Torture
36%

Were Torture
60%

Question: "Do you approve or disapprove of the Bush administration's decision to use these procedures while questioning suspected terrorists?"

Unsure
3%

Approve
50

Disapprove
46%

Taken from: CNN/Opinion Research Corporation Poll, April 23–26, 2009.

beaten or restrained in painful positions for hours, but the psychological suffering can be intense.

Such techniques are gruesome, dehumanizing and dangerous. Noted one torture victim I cared for at the Bellevue/NYU Program for Survivors of Torture in New York City, "As someone who has experienced torture, I know these things are torture." Clinical experience and data from the medical literature are clear. These techniques can cause significant and long lasting physical and psychological pain and harm. The patients my colleagues and I care for include many who were persecuted and tortured in countries whose regimes we have denounced. They describe forms of torture abuse eerily familiar to what Mr. Cheney and others label as "enhanced interrogations."

The Difference Between Torture and Training Exercises

In a [April 28, 2009] *Wall Street Journal* article entitled "Misconceptions about the Interrogation Memos" William McSwain a former Marine Commander and assistant U.S. attorney stated he was "none the worse for the wear" from waterboarding and sleep deprivation he endured as part of his Survival, Evasion, Resistance, Escape (SERE) training. Mr. Cheney's daughter, Lynn, in defense of her father has also referred to the SERE training as evidence that use of these methods are safe and legal. However, there is a profound difference between a soldier subjected to these methods in the context of military training, where they have every right to believe that they will not be harmed and a prisoner who has no such assurances. Furthermore, the SERE methods were never intended for eliciting the truth, but for training our soldiers how to resist torture. In fact these methods were adopted from the Chinese, Soviets and North Koreans who effectively used them to elicit false confessions. The morally and scientifically

> **FAST FACT**
>
> Interrogation techniques approved for use by the US military include yelling, sleep deprivation, waterboarding, the use of stress positions, multi-hour interrogations, controlled fear using animals, forced nudity, and other acts.

misguided reverse engineering of these methods occurred under the supervision of U.S. health professionals.

Not an Isolated Incident

Claims by Mr. Cheney and other former Bush Administration officials including former Attorney General [Michael] Mukasey, and former CIA Director [Michael] Hayden that such abusive methods were used only with high value detainees as a means of last resort, or were the unauthorized, sadistic practices of a few bad apples at Abu Ghraib, are inconsistent with substantial documentation to the contrary and fly in the face of common sense. Reports showed FBI officials who believed they were getting useful information from standard interrogation techniques refused to continue participating when abusive methods were used. The events at Abu Ghraib were the result of policies and leadership that permitted and in fact encouraged this kind of abuse. A 2008 *Physicians for Human Rights* report that I coauthored described detailed forensic examinations of 12 former Abu Ghraib and Guantanamo detainees. We found substantial evidence corroborating their reports of torture and the devastating health consequences. All of these former detainees were released after several years without being charged. It is likely that hundreds if not thousands of individuals were subjected to similar arbitrary imprisonment and abuses at these and other U.S. detention facilities including in Afghanistan and Eastern Europe.

When Mr. Cheney and others who claim that our national security is undermined by the U.S. unequivocally saying that we will treat prisoners in our custody humanely, then at least they should not look to whitewash the enhanced interrogation methods they hold up as necessary and effective, but instead call them what they are—torture.

Those Who Authorized Torture Should Be Prosecuted

The recently released memos detailing interrogation methods authorized by the Bush Administration, which by any reasonable standard constitute torture, demonstrate the critical need for an independent and comprehensive investigation into these Bush Administration policies and those responsible for them. Nothing less than our country's national security and stature as a leader in promoting human rights are at stake. Senate Judiciary Chair Patrick Leahy got it right when he said "We cannot continue to look the other way; we need to understand how these policies were formed if we are to ensure that this can never happen again."

The need for such an investigation is further demonstrated by Mr. Cheney's recent remarks in which he dismisses questions about Bush Administration interrogation policies as "nothing but feigned outrage based on a false narrative" and "contrived indignation and phony moralizing about the interrogation methods applied to "a few captured terrorists." Mr. Cheney further derides any calls for investigations:

> Some are even demanding that those who recommended and approved the interrogations be prosecuted, in effect, treating political disagreements as a punishable offense, and political opponents as criminals. It's hard to imagine a worse precedent, filled with more possibilities for trouble and abuse, than to have an incoming administration criminalize the policy decisions of its predecessors.

Just as Mr. Cheney's simplistic assertion that Abu Ghraib was caused by a few bad apples, he now seeks to equate any efforts at accountability as merely political "sour grapes." And while it may be easy to dismiss Mr. Cheney and his statements as marginalized, he is far from alone. On today's edition [May 26, 2009] of *Meet the Press*, former House Speaker Newt Gingrich also reiterated the false assertion that the "enhanced interrogation practices were only used in very limited circumstances." A full page ad that recently appeared in the *New York Times* by the "Torture Truth Project" called on the U.S. media to stop misleading the world that our country condones torture. Again it is the messenger rather than the perpetrator who gets blamed. And it isn't our country that condones torture, but rather our prior administration that condoned torture. This again demonstrates why investigation and accountability regarding torture are essential in demonstrating to the world that we are a country that functions under the rule of law and no one is above the law.

Torture Hurts Everyone

I appreciate that President Obama is inundated by pressing domestic and international concerns. Our economy, health care reform,

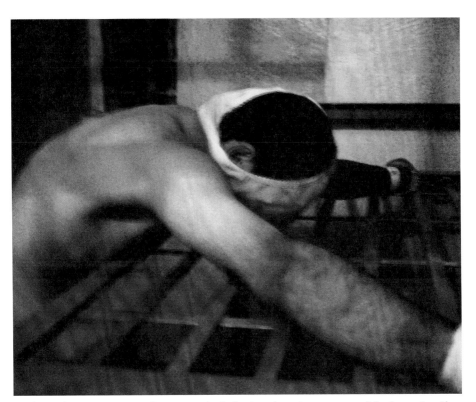

Enhanced interrogation techniques include forcing the prisoner to stand for hours (until the legs swell up and produce potentially life-threatening blood clots), forced nudity, and sexual humiliation.

the intensifying war in Afghanistan, and digging ourselves out of the horrible mire of Guantanamo created by the prior administration present enormous challenges. This too might seem good reason to move on, or leave it to the current investigative bodies including Congressional committees who have or will hold hearings, and the justice department to continue. But these separate investigations, will provide snapshots, rather than a much needed comprehensive overview. This is not about looking backward, but rather taking the necessary measures to prevent this from happening again. Such an investigation should also examine the roles that health professionals played in developing and implementing this policy of torture. Furthermore, the focus of this investigation should be on the senior policy makers and not simply the attorneys who wrote the legal memos justifying these policies or the rank and file agents and soldiers who implemented these policies.

Torture is neither reliable in eliciting accurate information nor in promoting national security. It is a violation of domestic and international law. Our use of torture has undermined our security and credibility including our capacity to speak out against despot regimes who routinely torture innocent civilians. An honest and full accounting of what happened is a crucial step in making this world a safer place.

> **EVALUATING THE AUTHORS' ARGUMENTS:**
>
> The author of the following viewpoint, A.W.R. Hawkins, is a conservative writer who holds a doctorate degree in US military history. Do you think Keller's hands-on experience with torture victims or Hawkins's academic credentials makes either one more credible than the other to debate the issue of torture? Explain your reasoning.

Enhanced Interrogation Techniques Are Not Torture

A.W.R. Hawkins

"The Obama administration is basically announcing to the world what we can and can't do if we catch a terrorist in the field or on the street."

In the following viewpoint, A.W.R. Hawkins argues that the harsh interrogation techniques allowed under the George W. Bush administration have been wrongly labeled as torture by politically correct liberals, including President Barack Obama. Hawkins suggests that restricting prisoner interrogation to the nineteen techniques listed in the *Army Field Manual* is too limiting, and dangerously compromises national security. Hawkins points out that the Army Field Manual has been made public, so enemy combatants can acquaint themselves with it and prepare themselves to withstand the methods described in it. Hawkins cites examples of prisoners giving up information when confronted with techniques not found in the *Army Field Manual* to make the point that useful information requires the use of enhanced interrogation techniques. Hawkins concludes that the United States

A.W.R. Hawkins, "Obama's Politically Correct Guide to War-Fighting," *Human Events,* January 27, 2009. Copyright © 2009 HUMAN EVENTS. All Rights Reserved. Reproduced by permission.

cannot take a politically correct approach to terrorists: rather, it must deal with them as harshly as they would deal with us.

A.W.R. Hawkins is a columnist for *Human Events* and holds a PhD in US military history from Texas Tech University.

AS YOU READ, CONSIDER THE FOLLOWING QUESTIONS:
1. What are "black sites," according to the author?
2. Who is John Cornyn, and how does he fit into the author's argument?
3. Who is Eric Holder, and how does he fit into the author's argument?

Simply put, from this point forward, [Barack] Obama is telling the CIA to interrogate terrorists that may be planning to blow up the crowded mall where your kids shop in the same way that our Army personnel interrogate a captured enemy soldier. Along the way, some of the techniques being categorized as "torture" to justify this policy are nothing more than "harsh techniques" (Obama's words), which politically-correct minds have conveniently labeled "torture."

The Army Field Manual lists among the interrogation techniques allowed: "Playing on a prisoner's anxieties, suggesting a prisoner may never see his family again if he refuses to cooperate, giving the prisoner the silent treatment, suggesting the prisoner may be punished for committing atrocities, posing rapid-fire questions, implying that the captors know all about the prisoner; 'False flag,' [which] involves tricking a detainee into believing he is the prisoner of another country's forces. [And] separation [which] may be used only on unlawful combatants." Among the interrogation techniques disallowed: "Waterboarding, Placing hoods or sacks over detainees' heads; using duct tape over their eyes; total sensory deprivation, [and the] use of military working dogs to intimidate detainees."

Since the Army Field Manual is available to the public, another problem with this politically correct–driven mess is that the Obama administration is basically announcing to the world what we can and can't do if we catch a terrorist in the field or on the street. This in itself takes away part of the force of our interrogations by giving would-be prisoners a heads up on our interrogating techniques.

When Michelle Oddis, Assistant Managing Editor of *Human Events*, interviewed Sen. Kit Bond (R-Mo) last week [in January 2009], he made this very point: "To limit interrogation techniques . . . [for] the intelligence agency, to [the] 19 techniques outlined in the army field manual, assures that high value al-Qaida people that [we] may catch in the future will know exactly what we can do." . . .

In addition to those problems, Sen. John Cornyn (R-Texas) points out that "because the techniques are unclassified [and therefore public], information from the [*Army Field Manual*] could be used by terrorists to resist interrogations." Did you catch that? Terrorists may so acquaint themselves with the techniques to which we've sworn to limit ourselves that they may be able to resist CIA interrogations when captured.

Bond demonstrated the need to drop this politically correct approach in another part of last week's interview with Oddis when he recalled "one detainee [on whom] we used some other techniques [not contained in the Army Field Manual]" during [George W.]"Bush's presidency. This particular detainee "was objecting because [the techniques] weren't in the field manual" but then "folded . . . when he found out that" Bush allowed "other techniques" to be used by interrogators.

Of course, Eric Holder, Obama's nominee for Attorney General, who just happens to have zero intelligence gathering experience, told the AP: "I'm not convinced at all that if we restrict ourselves to the Army field manual . . . we will be in any way less effective in the interrogation of people who have sworn to do us harm."

Contrast Holder's words with Bond's, and you get a totally different picture. Put them in context with the experience of someone who actually has hands-on experience in gathering intelligence. For example, former CIA officer John Kiriakou, who "was a member of the team that captured and [waterboarded] al-Qaida operative Abu Zubaydah in Pakistan in 2002" said "he believes that Zubaydah would have continued to refuse to talk if the technique hadn't been used. He also says he believes American lives were saved as a result of the information the CIA learned through the interrogation."

In other words, Kiriakou believes that if the CIA had been limited to the allowable techniques outlined in the Army Field Manual when interrogating Zubaydah, they never could have obtained information that saved lives.

I spoke to a former member of the U.S. military who was trained in Beirut, Lebanon and schooled in Arabic while there. On condition of anonymity, I asked about Obama's recent executive order, and he said: "If the CIA has to refer to the army manual, which is absolutely ridiculous to begin with, this is not going to work. Our government is not fighting back. It's like we've walked into a boxing ring and promised to keep our hands down at our sides while the other guy punches away." He closed the conversation by saying, "Terrorists will not be broken without exceeding the army field manual."

It seems that Obama's politically [correct] guide to war-fighting is a recipe for disaster.

EVALUATING THE AUTHOR'S ARGUMENTS:

A.W.R. Hawkins argues that the US needs to go outside the bounds of the *Army Field Manual* if it is to yield useful and life-saving information from suspected terrorists. Write 2-3 sentences on how you think each of the other authors in this chapter might respond to this position. Then, state your opinion on the matter, and make sure your answer contains at least one quote from the texts you have read.

Waterboarding Is Torture

Mark Benjamin

"This is revolting and it is deeply disturbing. . . . This fine-tuning of torture is unethical, incompetent and a disgrace to medicine."

In the following viewpoint, Mark Benjamin provides reasons why he believes waterboarding should be regarded as torture. Waterboarding is one of the enhanced interrogation techniques that was approved for use by the US government on captured and suspected terrorists. Intended to make them talk about terrorist plots, terrorist networks, and other such information, waterboarding, Benjamin claims, has caused detainees to stop breathing, choke on their own vomit, go into a coma, and even die. He says that the careful detail with which CIA officials have documented waterboarding problems and protocols is evidence of how akin to torture the technique is. Benjamin says that rather than being a harmless "dunk in the water," as proponents have described it, waterboarding is a brutal and dehumanizing form of torture.

Benjamin is a Washington, D.C.–based national correspondent for Salon.com, where this viewpoint was originally published.

Mark Benjamin, "Waterboarding for Dummies," *Salon.com,* March 9, 2010. This article first appeared in *Salon.com,* at http://www.Salon.com. An online version remains in the *Salon* archives. Reprinted with permission.

AS YOU READ, CONSIDER THE FOLLOWING QUESTIONS:

1. Who is Scott Allen and how does Benjamin incorporate him into his argument?
2. What is hyponatremia? How does it factor into the author's argument?
3. What is "psychological resignation," as described by the author?

Self-proclaimed waterboarding fan Dick Cheney called it a no-brainer in a 2006 radio interview: Terror suspects should get a "a dunk in the water." But recently released internal documents reveal the controversial "enhanced interrogation" practice was far more brutal on detainees than Cheney's description sounds, and was administered with meticulous cruelty.

Interrogators pumped detainees full of so much water that the CIA turned to a special saline solution to minimize the risk of death, the documents show. The agency used a gurney "specially designed" to tilt backwards at a perfect angle to maximize the water entering the prisoner's nose and mouth, intensifying the sense of choking—and to be lifted upright quickly in the event that a prisoner stopped breathing.

The documents also lay out, in chilling detail, exactly what should occur in each two-hour waterboarding "session." Interrogators were instructed to start pouring water right after a detainee exhaled, to ensure he inhaled water, not air, in his next breath. They could use their hands to "dam the runoff" and prevent water from spilling out of a detainee's mouth. They were allowed six separate 40-second "applications" of liquid in each two-hour session—and could dump water over a detainee's nose and mouth for a total of 12 minutes a day. Finally, to keep detainees alive even if they inhaled their own vomit during a session—a not-uncommon side effect of waterboarding—the prisoners were kept on a liquid diet. The agency recommended Ensure Plus.

"This is revolting, and it is deeply disturbing," said Dr. Scott Allen, co-director of the Center for Prisoner Health and Human Rights at Brown University who has reviewed all of the documents for Physicians for Human Rights. "The so-called science here is a total departure from any ethics or any legitimate purpose. They are saying, 'This is how risky and harmful the procedure is, but we are still going to do it.' It just sounds like lunacy," he said. "This fine-tuning of torture is unethical, incompetent and a disgrace to medicine."

These torture guidelines were contained in a ream of internal government documents made public over the past year, including a legal review of Bush–era CIA interrogations by the Justice Department's Office of Professional Responsibility released late last month.

Though public, the hundreds of pages of documents authorizing or later reviewing the agency's "enhanced interrogation program" haven't been mined for waterboarding details until now. While Bush-Cheney officials defended the legality and safety of waterboarding by noting the practice has been used to train U.S. service members to resist torture, the documents show that the agency's methods went far beyond anything ever done to a soldier during training. U.S. soldiers, for example, were generally waterboarded with a cloth over their face one time, never more than twice, for about 20 seconds, the CIA admits in its own documents.

Demonstrators hold a mock waterboarding to protest a practice that they believe is torture.

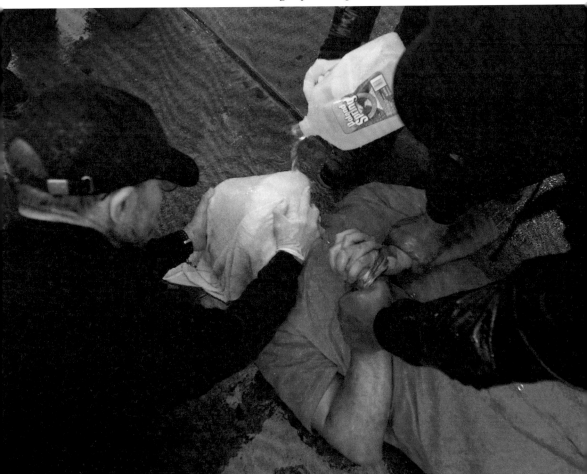

(After this story was published, Salon learned that Marcy Wheeler, the author of the blog Emptywheel, and several other bloggers have written about many of the documents released over the past year.)

These memos show the CIA went much further than that with terror suspects, using huge and dangerous quantities of liquid over long periods of time. The CIA's waterboarding was "different" from training for elite soldiers, according to the Justice Department document released last month. "The difference was in the manner in which the detainee's breathing was obstructed," the document notes. In soldier training, "The interrogator applies a small amount of water to the cloth (on a soldier's face) in a controlled manner," DOJ wrote. "By contrast, the agency interrogator . . . continuously applied large volumes of water to a cloth that covered the detainee's mouth and nose."

One of the more interesting revelations in the documents is the use of a saline solution in waterboarding. Why? Because the CIA forced such massive quantities of water into the mouths and noses of detainees, prisoners inevitably swallowed huge amounts of liquid—enough to conceivably kill them from hyponatremia, a rare but deadly condition in which ingesting enormous quantities of water results in a dangerously low concentration of sodium in the blood. Generally a concern only for marathon runners, who on extremely rare occasions drink that much water, hyponatremia could set in during a prolonged waterboarding session. A waterlogged, sodium-deprived prisoner might become confused and lethargic, slip into convulsions, enter a coma and die.

Therefore, "based on advice of medical personnel," Principal Deputy Assistant Attorney General Steven Bradbury wrote in a May 10, 2005, memo authorizing continued use of waterboarding, "the CIA requires that saline solution be used instead of plain water to reduce the possibility of hyponatremia."

The agency used so much water there was also another risk: pneumonia resulting from detainees inhaling the fluid forced into their mouths and noses. Saline, the CIA argued, might reduce the risk of pneumonia when this occurred.

"The detainee might aspirate some of the water, and the resulting water in the lungs might lead to pneumonia," Bradbury noted in the same memo. "To mitigate this risk, a potable saline solution is used in the procedure."

That particular Bradbury memo laid out a precise and disturbing protocol for what went on in each waterboarding session. The CIA used a "specially designed" gurney for waterboarding, Bradbury wrote. After immobilizing a prisoner by strapping him down, interrogators then tilted the gurney to a 10–15 degree downward angle, with the detainee's head at the lower end. They put a black cloth over his face and poured water, or saline, from a height of 6 to 18 inches, documents show. The slant of the gurney helped drive the water more directly into the prisoner's nose and mouth. But the gurney could also be tilted upright quickly, in the event the prisoner stopped breathing.

Detainees would be strapped to the gurney for a two-hour "session." During that session, the continuous flow of water onto a detainee's face was not supposed to exceed 40 seconds during each pour. Interrogators could perform six separate 40-second pours during each session, for a total of four minutes of pouring. Detainees could be subjected to two of those two-hour sessions during a 24-hour period, which adds up to eight minutes of pouring. But the

FAST FACT

A May 2009 CNN poll found that six in ten Americans believe waterboarding amounts to torture.

CIA's guidelines say interrogators could pour water over the nose and mouth of a detainne for 12 minutes total during each 24-hour period. The documents do not explain the extra four minutes to get to 12.

Interrogators were instructed to pour the water when a detainee had just exhaled so that he would inhale during the pour. An interrogator was also allowed to force the water down a detainee's mouth and nose using his hands. "The interrogator may cup his hands around the detainee's nose and mouth to dam the runoff," the Bradbury memo notes. "In which case it would not be possible for the detainee to breathe during the application of the water."

"We understand that water may enter—and accumulate in—the detainee's mouth and nasal cavity, preventing him from breathing," the memo admits.

Should a prisoner stop breathing during the procedure, the documents instructed interrogators to rapidly tilt the gurney to an upright position to expel the saline. "If the detainee is not breathing freely

Most Americans Consider Waterboarding Torture

A 2009 poll revealed that regardless of whether they supported its use, the overwhelming majority of Americans consider waterboarding torture.

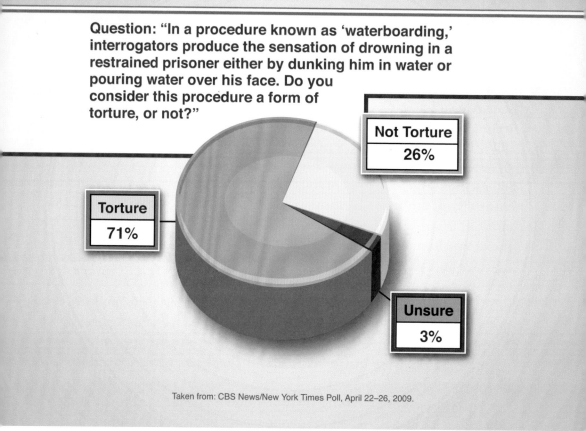

Question: "In a procedure known as 'waterboarding,' interrogators produce the sensation of drowning in a restrained prisoner either by dunking him in water or pouring water over his face. Do you consider this procedure a form of torture, or not?"

Not Torture
26%

Torture
71%

Unsure
3%

Taken from: CBS News/New York Times Poll, April 22–26, 2009.

after the cloth is removed from his face, he is immediately moved to a vertical position in order to clear the water from this mouth, nose, and nasopharynx," Bradbury wrote. "The gurney used for administering this technique is specially designed so that this can be accomplished very quickly if necessary."

Documents drafted by CIA medical officials in 2003, about a year after the agency started using the waterboard, describe more aggressive procedures to get water out of the subject breathing. "An unresponsive subject should be righted immediately," the CIA Office of Medical Services ordered in its Sept. 4, 2003, medical guidelines for interrogations. "The interrogator should then deliver a sub-xyphoid thrust to expel the water." (That's a blow below the sternum, similar to the thrust delivered to a choking victum in the Heimlich maneuver.)

But even those steps might not force the prisoner to resume breathing. Waterboarding, according to the Bradbury memo, could produce "spasms of the larynx" that might keep a prisoner from breathing "even when the application of water is stopped and the detainee is returned to an upright position." In such cases, Bradbury wrote, "a qualified physician would immediately intervene to address the problem and, if necessary, the intervening physician would perform a tracheotomy." The agency required that "necessary emergency medial equipment" be kept readily available for the procedure. The documents do not say if doctors ever performed a tracheotomy on a prisoner.

The doctors were also present to monitor the detainee "to ensure the at the does not develop respiratory distress." A leaked 2007 report from the International Committee of the Red Cross says that meant the detainee's finger was fixed with a pulse oxymeter, a device that measures the oxygen saturation level in the blood during the procedure. Doctors like Allen say this would allow interrogators to push a detainee close to death—but help them from crossing the line. "It is measuring in real time the oxygen content in the blood second by second," Allen explained about the pulse oxymeter. "It basically allows them to push these prisoners more to the edge. With that, you can keep going. This is a calibration of harm by health professionals."

One of the weirdest details in the documents is the revelation that the agency placed detainees on liquid diets prior to the use of waterboarding. That's because during waterboarding, "a detainee might vomit and then aspirate the emesis," Bradbury wrote. In other words, breathe in his own vomit. The CIA recommended the use of Ensure Plus for the liquid diet.

Plowing through hundreds of pages of these documents is an unsettling experience. On one level, the detailed instructions can be seen as helping to carry out kinder, gentler waterboarding, with so much care and attention given to making sure detainees didn't stop breathing, get pneumonia, breathe in their own vomit or die. But of course dead detainees tell no tales, so the CIA needed to keep many of its prisoners alive. It should be noted, though, that six human rights groups in 2007 released a report showing that 39 people who appeared to have gone into the CIA's secret prison network haven't shown up since. The careful attention to detail in the documents was also used to provide legal cover for the harsh and probably illegal interrogation tactics.

As brutal as the waterbording process was, the memos also reveal that the Bush-era Justice Department authorized the CIA to use it in combination with other forms of torture. Specifically, a detainee could be kept awake for more than seven days straight by shackling his hands in a standing position to a bolt in the ceiling so he could never sit down. The agency diapered and hand-fed its detainees during this period before putting them on the waterboard. Another memo from Bradbury, also from 2005, says that in between waterboarding sessions, a detainee could be physically slammed into a wall, crammed into a small box, placed in "stress positions" to increase discomfort and doused with cold water, among other things.

The CIA's waterboarding regimen was so excruciating, the memos show, that agency officials found themselves grappling with an unexpected development: detainees simply gave up and tried to let themselves drown. "In our limited experience, extensive sustained use of the waterboard can introduce new risks," the CIA's Office of Medical Services wrote in its 2003 memo. "Most seriously, for reasons of physical fatigue or psychological resignation, the subject may simply give up, allowing excessive filling of the airways and loss of consciousness."

The agency's medical guidelines say that after a case of "psychological resignation" by a detainee on the waterboard, an interrogator had to get approval from a CIA doctor before doing it again.

The memo also contains a last, little-noticed paragraph that may be the most disturbing of all. It seems to say that the detainees subjected to waterboarding were also guinea pigs. The language is eerily reminiscent of the very reasons the Nuremberg Code was written in the first place. The paragraph reads as follows:

"NOTE: In order to best inform future medical judgments and recommendations, it is important that every application of the waterboard be thoroughly documented: how long each application (and the entire procedure) lasted, how much water was used in the process (realizing that much splashes off), how exactly the water was applied, if a seal was achieved, if the naso- or oropharynx was filled, what sort of volume was expelled, how long was the break between applications, and how the subject looked between each treatment."

EVALUATING THE AUTHOR'S ARGUMENTS:

In this viewpoint, Mark Benjamin details the process of waterboarding in order to argue that it should be viewed as torture. After reading his account, and given what you know on the topic, do you think it is acceptable to subject captured and suspected terrorists to waterboarding? Why or why not? Quote from the texts you have read in your answer.

Viewpoint
4

Waterboarding Is Not Torture

Joseph Farah

"A few seconds of dripping water on a prisoner's face? That's not torture to me."

Joseph Farah is a nationally syndicated columnist. In the following viewpoint he explains why waterboarding should not be regarded as torture. Waterboarding is an unpleasant but safe technique that is used judiciously and with responsible supervision, he says. It is so benign, in fact, Farah says, that America's own soldiers undergo waterboarding as part of their training. Real torture, according to Farah, involves cutting off limbs or gouging out a prisoner's eyes. Farah concludes that waterboarding is unpleasant enough to make captured terrorists talk, but not unpleasant enough to qualify as torture. He urges Americans to retain the use of the technique so they can thwart future terrorist plots.

AS YOU READ, CONSIDER THE FOLLOWING QUESTIONS:
1. Who "sang like canaries" after being waterboarded, according to Farah?
2. How does the fact that so few Americans have experienced combat factor into the author's argument?
3. What is Farah's definition of torture? What does it involve?

Joseph Farah, "Waterboarding Is Not Torture," *Human Events,* 2008. Reprinted by permission.

Americans simply are losing their ability to distinguish right from wrong.

I don't know how else to put it. Up is down, day is night, left is right and right is wrong. A good illustration of my thesis is the growing political consensus around the idea that the U.S. should stop using any effective interrogation techniques that make our terrorist enemies uncomfortable—even those terrorists who were involved in planning acts of mass destruction and annihilation. For instance, armchair generals increasingly are referring to waterboarding as torture and saying it must be stopped in all cases.

We Need to Waterboard Our Enemies

I have no doubt that waterboarding is a very unpleasant experience. It must be so because it is considered 100 percent effective and usually induces cooperation within 30 seconds.

The technique of waterboarding involves pouring water on the head of a prisoner with the purpose of triggering a gag reflex and the panic of imminent drowning.

It was used successfully to learn about terrorist operations planned by two of al-Qaida's top operatives: Khalid Sheikh Mohammed, involved in the planning of the Sept. 11 [2001] attacks, and Abu Zubaida, another leader of the terrorist organization.

Apparently both of these mass killers endured many hours of coercive interrogations without talking. But they sang like canaries after a few seconds of waterboarding. In both cases, there is reason to believe planned terrorist attacks were foiled as a result of this technique.

Nevertheless, there is a growing chorus of opposition against any further use of waterboarding in similar or even direr scenarios.

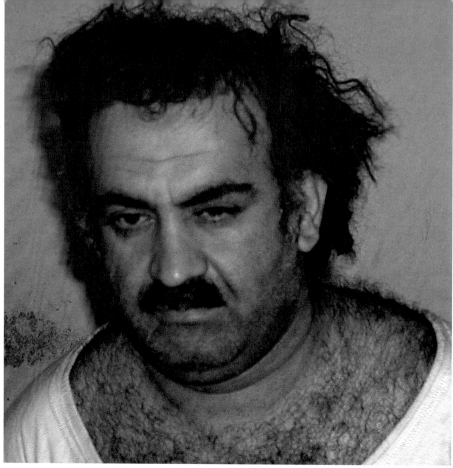

Waterboarding was used on Khalid Sheikh Mohammad and as a result, he revealed plans of al Qaeda terrorist operations.

Waterboarding Saves Lives

Let's use our heads for a minute. Imagine American law enforcement or military authorities have captured a terrorist mastermind who has knowledge about an imminent nuclear detonation in an unknown American city. He knows the time, the location and the details about the warhead. The bomb could be going off at any minute. It could kill hundreds of thousands of innocent people.

Would you really want waterboarding to be banned under all circumstances? What alternatives would you suggest for quick results? Should we call in top negotiators from the State Department? Should we play loud rap music? Should we force the prisoner to listen to [Secretary of State] Hillary Rodham Clinton speeches? While I also find those experiences unpleasant, I don't think they would produce the needed results in time to defuse the bomb.

Let's not tie the hands of future Jack Bauers [from the TV show *24*] who will need to do what they have to do to save lives.

We Are Confused About What Constitutes Torture

I personally think Mohammed and Zubaida got off way too easy with waterboarding. I would have performed far more unpleasant procedures on them without a twinge of guilt in my conscience. Real torture techniques would have been appropriate in both cases.

Here's why waterboarding is *not* torture:

Do you know the U.S. military waterboards hundreds of our own soldiers every year? It is part of the conditioning Special Forces troops undergo to prepare for battle and the possibility of capture by the enemy. In other words, it's OK for us to do this to America's best and brightest, but it's too horrible for our worst enemies? Does this make sense to anyone?

Many Americans are simply confused about the real definition of torture. Because so little sacrifice is required of most Americans today and because so few have experienced combat, they equate momentary discomfort or fear with torture. They are not the same. My definition of torture is simple: It involves physical or mental abuse that leaves lasting scars. Cutting off fingers, toes, limbs—that would be torture. Forcing prisoners to play Russian roulette—that would be torture. Sticking hot pokers in the eyes of prisoners—that would be torture.

But a few seconds of dripping water on a prisoner's face? That's not torture to me.

> ### EVALUATING THE AUTHORS' ARGUMENTS:
>
> Farah characterizes waterboarding as "a few seconds of dripping water on a prisoner's face." How do you think Mark Benjamin, author of the previous viewpoint, would respond to this characterization? After reading both viewpoints, with which author do you agree—does waterboarding qualify as torture? Explain your reasoning.

The Death Penalty Is a Form of Torture

> "It's sad that we live in a society where there are more mandatory regulations for euthanizing animals than there are for executing human beings."

Stanley Howard

In the following viewpoint, Stanley Howard argues that the death penalty constitutes cruel and unusual punishment, and is akin to torture. He discusses a botched execution in which a prisoner's death was painfully extended and unable to be carried out because executioners could not find a vein in which to inject a fatal dose of medication. The execution went on for so long, says Howard, the prisoner had to help his executioners attempt to kill him. The author describes this scene as both physical and mental torture. He concludes that the death penalty is immoral for several reasons, most of all because it is wrong to subject even convicted killers to something so cruel and inhumane as legalized torture and murder.

Howard is a former Illinois death row prisoner who was exonerated and pardoned on murder charges in 2003, although he remains incarcerated on armed robbery

Stanley Howard, "More than a Botched Execution," *Socialist Worker,* November 18, 2009. Reprinted by permission.

charges. He continues to claim his innocence and writes for the *New Abolitionist*, the newsletter of the Campaign to End the Death Penalty.

AS YOU READ, CONSIDER THE FOLLOWING QUESTIONS:
1. Who is Romell Broom, as described by the author? List at least three facts about him.
2. According to Howard, what do sick animals enjoy that human beings in the United States do not?
3. What does the word "commute" mean in the context of the viewpoint?

The writing is on the wall for an end to the death penalty in America. But unfortunately, stubborn government officials around the country continue ignoring the overwhelming evidence proving that the system is unjust, racist, broken and barbaric.

I had George W. Bush, the Texecutioner when he was governor of Texas, at the top of my list of officials willing to say or do anything to maintain the status quo and public confidence in a system that should be dismantled.

He executed over 150 men and women in a short five-year span. And when the validity of some of those executions came under fire, Bush foolishly proclaimed that he was positive "every one of them was guilty," because he personally reviewed each case. Anyone who knows anything about the criminal justice system knows that it's impossible for him to be so certain.

FAST FACT

The Death Penalty Information Center reports there have been at least forty-three botched executions in the United States since 1982.

But Ohio Gov. Ted Strickland has taken this stubbornness to an all-time low.

Helping Their Executioners to Make the Torture End
On September 15, 2009, an execution team at the Southern Ohio Correctional Facility in Lucasville, tortured Romell Broom for over

Death Penalty in the United States

The majority of US states retain the death penalty, but it remains among America's most controversial social issues.

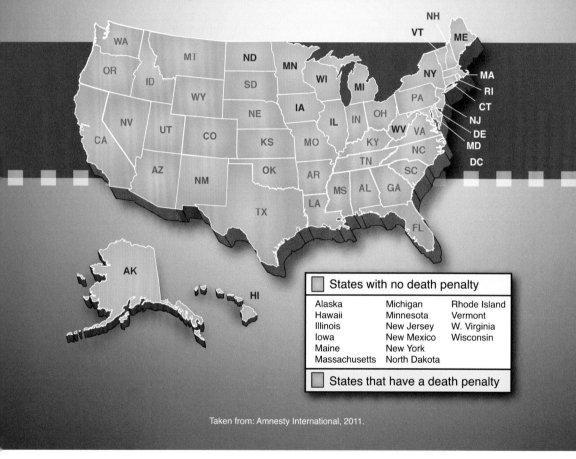

States with no death penalty

Alaska	Michigan	Rhode Island
Hawaii	Minnesota	Vermont
Illinois	New Jersey	W. Virginia
Iowa	New Mexico	Wisconsin
Maine	New York	
Massachusetts	North Dakota	

States that have a death penalty

Taken from: Amnesty International, 2011.

two hours, trying to administer the drugs used to kill Ohio's condemned prisoners.

Numerous attempts were made to find a suitable vein as the 53-year-old Broom winced in pain each time the needle pierced his skin. The pain got so unbearable that Broom actually tried to assist his executioners by pointing out veins. He even turned over on his side to provide access to other parts of his body.

When I was on Illinois death row, I had my mind set on being disruptive, and making it hard as hell for them to execute me. I wasn't going to participate in the process in any manner. I actually dreamed of trying to stop them from executing me—fighting and screaming that I was innocent.

I cannot imagine lying on a gurney in the death chamber, most likely an emotional wreck and on the verge of going into shock, having to help my executioners to execute me. But if I were being physically and mentally tortured—like Broom and Stanley Tookie Williams, who was executed in California in 2005—I probably would help to accelerate the process to stop from being tortured to death.

Even Murderers Have Rights

Gov. Strickland issued a temporary reprieve due to the failed attempt, and Broom's lawyers petitioned the courts to stop Ohio from getting a second chance at taking his life. The lawyers are arguing that a second attempt would amount to cruel and unusual punishment.

This is the third botched execution Ohio has had in recent years, and there's no guarantee that they will not botch another attempt at taking Broom's life, or botch one of their upcoming executions.

Because of these possibilities, Strickland promised to look into the circumstances surrounding Broom's failed execution, but believes it isn't necessary to review the entire process. He decided to delay four other scheduled executions until the problems, if there are any problems, are resolved.

Prosecutors and others point to the cruelty of Broom's alleged crime, the rape and murder of a 14-year-old girl, to justify going forth with the second attempt—regardless of how cruel and inhumane it would be.

There's no doubt that punishment must be levied against the perpetrators of such atrocities. But it's sad that we live in a society where there are more mandatory regulations for euthanizing animals than there are for executing human beings. It's hard to believe that in America—the so-called "human rights champion of the world"—we are willing to go to any cruel length to obtain vengeance and retribution against such perpetrators.

As governor of Texas, George W. Bush executed over 150 Texas men and woman in a five-year span.

There Is No Humane Way to Kill

Gov. Strickland should not turn a blind eye to this barbaric policy and practice of state-sanctioned murder. He should come to the realization that there is no humane way of killing a healthy human being.

And because it's no longer politically dangerous for a governor to take action to prevent a miscarriage of justice or to show compassion in death penalty cases, Strickland should commute the death sentences of Broom and all of Ohio's death row prisoners.

EVALUATING THE AUTHOR'S ARGUMENTS:

The author of this viewpoint was wrongfully convicted of murder. He served sixteen years in prison before the governor of Illinois pardoned him after he was proved innocent. Does knowing Howard's personal experience with this issue make you more likely to agree with him that the death penalty constitutes torture? If so, why? If not, why not?

The Death Penalty Is Not a Form of Torture

"The death penalty, far from being a form of state-sanctioned viciousness, actually demonstrates greater compassion to both murderers and victims."

Colin Wilson

In the following viewpoint, Colin Wilson explains why he thinks the death penalty is not a form of torture. In his opinion, the death penalty is humane because it offers convicted killers a swift and merciful death, whereas life in prison offers them a mentally and physically torturous existence that often ends badly. Indeed, according to Wilson, it is life in prison that constitutes a form of torture. He maintains that living indefinitely in prison subjects inmates to the cruelty, violence, and bloodthirstiness of other inmates, and also makes them prone to multiple failed suicide attempts that can render them paralyzed, comatose, or otherwise worse off. Wilson concludes that the death penalty is a compassionate and moral way to deal with society's worst criminals.

Wilson is a British author whose articles have appeared in the *Daily Mail*, where this viewpoint was originally published.

Colin Wilson, "Hanging Ian Huntley Would Have Been More Humane," *Daily Mail* (UK), March 23, 2010. Reprinted by permission.

AS YOU READ, CONSIDER THE FOLLOWING QUESTIONS:
1. Who is Ian Huntley? What happened to him in prison, and how does this event factor into Wilson's argument?
2. What, according to Wilson, is grotesque and inhumane about incarcerating elderly inmates?
3. What would a truly moral society be wise to recognize, according to Wilson?

When D. Harold Shipman, the worst serial killer in British history, committed suicide in 2004, the Home Secretary of the time David Blunkett confessed his first instinct on hearing the news was to 'open a bottle' [that is, to celebrate].

No doubt many felt the same way when they learnt that double child murderer Ian Huntley had been badly slashed across the throat in prison by a fellow inmate.

Any sense of regret would be caused not by concern over Huntley's injuries, but the fact that his attacker failed to complete the job.

Yet, in the wake of Shipman's death, Blunkett also expressed his surprise at a widespread feeling of public anger that the murderous doctor had somehow cheated justice by taking his own life.

As Blunkett pointed out, there was a mood that Shipman had avoided the punishment that he deserved, namely a lifetime behind bars.

Suicide was the easy way out for him. According to this argument, decade upon decade in a solitary cell was the fate Shipman merited, not a swift, sudden end.

The same sense of frustrated vengeance was obvious when monstrous mass murderer Fred West was found hanged in his jail in 1995.

And no doubt the same bitterness would have arisen if Ian Huntley had succeeded in any of the three suicide bids he has made since he was locked up in 2004 or if his wounds from the recent assault had proved fatal. That, by escaping a long sentence, Huntley would have somehow avoided paying for his terrible crimes.

The Death Penalty Is Not Cruel Enough
This points to a fascinating paradox at the heart of public attitudes towards the punishment of the worst murderers.

Convicted murderer Ian Huntley tried committing suicide three times and was assaulted by a fellow prisoner. Death penalty proponents believe it is less cruel to execute him than for him to spend the rest of his life in prison.

We like to think our society is more humane that those of the past. Unlike our ancestors, we no longer wallow in barbarity. The ultimate symbol of this spirit of compassion, we are led to believe, has been the abolition of capital punishment.

Yet in direct contradiction of this outlook, there is a sense that in cases like Huntley's and Shipman's, the death penalty is not cruel enough and that execution does not match the magnitude of the crimes.

It is a viewpoint reflected in sayings such as 'hanging's too good for him' or 'lock him up and throw away the key'.

I have always found it curious that people who see opposition to the death penalty as a badge of their liberal humanity should be so enthusiastic about inhumanly long prison sentences.

In reality, the death penalty, far from being a form of state-sanctioned viciousness, actually demonstrates greater compassion to both murderer and victims.

The Death Penalty Is More Compassionate Than Other Sentences

For the killer, the gallows are surely less terrible than the lingering twilight existence of permanent incarceration. Indeed, the suicides of West and Shipman are proof of this, while Ian Brady, the Moors murderer [of five children] who has been locked up for more than 40 years, has been pleading for the last decade to be executed.

Brady, whom I know fairly well from ten years of correspondence, has grasped the full horror of a lifetime behind bars and wants an end to the nightmare.

Before the abolition of the death penalty [in the UK] in 1965, the penal system did not have to cope with the problem of elderly inmates without hope of ever gaining freedom. But now we have a growing number of 'lifers' who will stay inside until their deaths.

There is nothing remotely humane about this grotesque phenomenon, especially when such inmates need permanent nursing care or suffer from dementia. Hanging would have been more civilised.

The death penalty is also more compassionate towards the victims of crime, who are able to move on with their lives.

> **FAST FACT**
>
> More than half of all American states—thirty-four as of 2011—have legalized the death penalty. The death penalty is also authorized by the federal government and the US military.

Americans Do Not View the Death Penalty as Torture

Americans have supported the death penalty for most of the time it has been legal. The majority consider it a just and humane way to deal with society's worst criminals.

Are you in favor of the death penalty for a person convicted of murder?

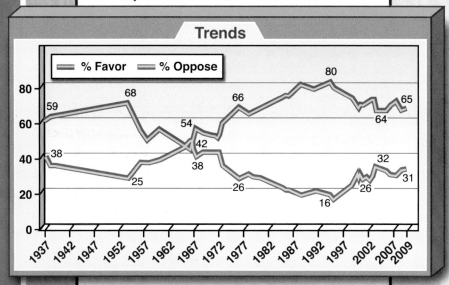

Trends

Specific Years	% For	% Against
2009	65	31
2008	64	30
2007	69	27
2006	67	28
2005	64	30
2004	64	31
2003	64	32
2002	70	25

2001	68	26
2000	66	26
1999	71	22
1995	77	13
1994	80	16
1991	76	18
1988	79	16
1986	70	22
1985	72	20
1981	66	25
1978	62	27
1976	66	26
1972	50	41
1971	49	40
1969	51	40
1967	54	38
1966	42	47
1965	45	43
1960	53	36
1957	47	34
1956	53	34
1953	68	25
1937	60	33
1936	59	38

*Percentage undecided not represented.

Taken from: Gallup Poll, October 2009.

Huntley might be released in 2042 on his completion of a 40-year sentence, if he lives that long. Such an eventuality can only cause further pain to the families of Holly Wells and Jessica Chapman.

And I fear that it would still be dangerous to release Huntley even when he is in his seventies because, as with other sex killers, he is likely still to be a compulsive predator. Again, this only shows how it would have been much better for society if Huntley had been hanged.

Life in Prison Is a Form of Torture

The long-standing practical objection to the death penalty, that it may lead to the death of an innocent man, is far weaker now thanks to advances in DNA technology. With someone like Huntley, there has never been a shred of doubt about his guilt.

The supposed miscarriage of justice always cited by opponents of execution is James Hanratty, who was hanged in 1962 for the A6 murder.[1]

Subsequent concerns about his guilt helped to drive the abolition of the death penalty three years later. It is a rich irony that modern DNA techniques have proved that Hanratty was not remotely innocent. Like most dangerous murderers, he thoroughly deserved to hang.

And that should have been the fate of Ian Huntley.

A truly moral society would recognise that no purpose is served by keeping him inside, little more than the object of target practice for other bloodthirsty prisoners and a psychotic maelstrom of his own suicidal fantasies.

EVALUATING THE AUTHORS' ARGUMENTS:

Colin Wilson and Stanley Howard (author of the previous viewpoint) disagree with each other on whether the death penalty constitutes a form of torture. In your opinion, which author made the better argument? Why? List at least three pieces of evidence (quotes, statistics, facts, or statements of reasoning) that caused you to side with one author over the other.

1. In which Michael Gregsten was killed.

Chapter 3

What Should US Policy on Torture Be?

Attorney General Eric Holder testified before the Senate Judiciary Committee that waterboarding was torture and the Bush administration had violated the law. However, Holder declined to charge any Bush official with war crimes.

US Officials Should Be Prosecuted for Sanctioning the Use of Torture

Doug Bandow

"The only way to prevent this from happening again is to make sure that those who were responsible for the torture program pay the price for it."

In the following viewpoint, Doug Bandow argues it was illegal for US officials to allow captured and suspected terrorists to be tortured. Therefore, he thinks these officials should be brought to justice. Bandow explains that several international treaties that the United States has signed make it illegal to sanction torture. He also says that America's use of torture has left it less safe, tarnished its global reputation, and hurt its moral standing. For these reasons, Bandow says US officials who sanctioned torture betrayed their country and ought to be punished for doing so. Prosecuting officials is the only way the country can move forward, says Bandow, and the best way to ensure that such a betrayal never happens again. Bandow predicts that the process of

Doug Bandow, "Investigate and Prosecute the Bush Administration," Antiwar.com, January 24, 2009. Reprinted by permission.

prosecuting US officials for torture will be difficult but ultimately is in the best interests of the country.

Bandow is a senior fellow at the Cato Institute, a think tank that specializes in foreign policy and civil liberties issues.

AS YOU READ, CONSIDER THE FOLLOWING QUESTIONS:
1. Who is Antonio M. Taguba and how does he factor into the author's argument?
2. What two documents has the United States ratified that Bandow suggests make it legally obligated to investigate those who sanctioned torture?
3. What does the word "deterrence" mean in the context of the viewpoint?

Not all presidential errors are merely questions of policy or politics. Some are matters of the law. The criminal law. . . . Presumably the [George W.] Bush administration believed that it was acting legally [when it sanctioned the use of "enhanced interrogation techniques"]. Genuine belief by officials that their conduct was legal might militate against prosecution, but alone should not be enough to insulate illegal and unconstitutional behavior. High government officials must be held accountable for their actions. Otherwise future officials will realize that they can violate the law with impunity by simply claiming that they believed the law to [be] on their side. . . .

Why Torture Is Illegal

[An] obvious violation of the law is the use of torture. The argument against torture is powerful: claims that "enhanced interrogation" methods, as the administration preferred to call its practices, remain unproven assertions. In fact, counter-terrorism officials familiar with the most noted cases discount the information acquired as a result of torture. In general, they dismiss the value of intelligence procured under duress and emphasize alternative strategies for getting information. Even FBI Director Robert Mueller admitted that he didn't

A Torture Chain of Command

Those who support the prosecution of US officials for sanctioning torture say the following people and institutions should be held responsible.

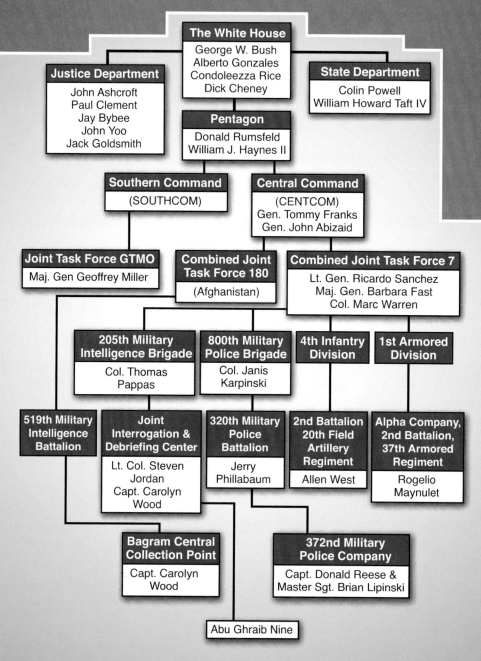

The White House
George W. Bush
Alberto Gonzales
Condoleezza Rice
Dick Cheney

Justice Department
John Ashcroft
Paul Clement
Jay Bybee
John Yoo
Jack Goldsmith

State Department
Colin Powell
William Howard Taft IV

Pentagon
Donald Rumsfeld
William J. Haynes II

Southern Command
(SOUTHCOM)

Central Command
(CENTCOM)
Gen. Tommy Franks
Gen. John Abizaid

Joint Task Force GTMO
Maj. Gen Geoffrey Miller

Combined Joint Task Force 180
(Afghanistan)

Combined Joint Task Force 7
Lt. Gen. Ricardo Sanchez
Maj. Gen. Barbara Fast
Col. Marc Warren

205th Military Intelligence Brigade
Col. Thomas Pappas

800th Military Police Brigade
Col. Janis Karpinski

4th Infantry Division

1st Armored Division

519th Military Intelligence Battalion

Joint Interrogation & Debriefing Center
Lt. Col. Steven Jordan
Capt. Carolyn Wood

320th Military Police Battalion
Jerry Phillabaum

2nd Battalion 20th Field Artillery Regiment
Allen West

Alpha Company, 2nd Battalion, 37th Armored Regiment
Rogelio Maynulet

Bagram Central Collection Point
Capt. Carolyn Wood

372nd Military Police Company
Capt. Donald Reese &
Master Sgt. Brian Lipinski

Abu Ghraib Nine

Taken from: Slate.com, May 26, 2005.

"believe it to be the case" that the Bush administration's tough interrogation practices prevented any terrorist attacks in the U.S.

Moreover, torture tarnishes America's global reputation, threatening Washington's ability to win the cooperation of friendly states in fighting terrorism. The practice also puts American forces at risk. A former special intelligence operations officer writing in the *Washington Post* under the pseudonym Matthew Alexander argued after his experience in Iraq: "It's no exaggeration to say that at least half of our losses and casualties in [Iraq] have come at the hands of foreigners who joined the fray because of our program of detainee abuse."

Finally, torture erodes America's moral core, so critical to what makes America worth defending. Notes Charles Fried of Harvard Law School, who also served as Solicitor General under President Ronald Reagan: "we cannot authorize indecency without jeopardizing our survival as a decent society.". . .

US Officials Committed War Crimes

If President Bush believed that he lacked sufficient authority under the law to protect America, he should have proposed that Congress amend or repeal the law. He did not have the option to ignore it.

Of course, the Bush administration repeatedly said that it did not torture—less than a week before leaving office, White House Press Secretary Dana Perino emphasized: "Let me just make sure it's clear—and I'll say it on the record one more time—that it has never been the policy of this president or this administration to torture." But the contrary evidence is overwhelming. The fact that congressional Democrats were regularly briefed on the administration's tactics spreads the blame rather than legitimizes the tactic.

Did the administration utilize torture? Don't ask liberal critics of the Bush regime. Ask Jack Goldsmith, who headed the Office of Legal Counsel and revoked two earlier legal opinions authorizing coercive interrogation. Ask retired Lt. Gen. Antonio M. Taguba, tasked by the Pentagon with investigating the Abu Ghraib scandal.[1] "There is no longer any doubt as to whether the current administration has committed war crimes. The only question that remains to be answered is

---

1. In which US soldiers abused Iraqi prisoners of war.

whether those who ordered the use of torture will be held to account." Ask Robert Turner, a Reagan White House attorney who said that war crimes "may well have been committed." Ask Susan Crawford, a retired judge (and Republican) appointed by the Defense Department to decide whether to charge Guantanamo Bay [detention camp, a U.S. facility located on Cuba] inmates. She called the treatment of one Saudi inmate torture, contending: "The buck stops in the Oval Office."

In short, detainees were tortured. The only questions are how many people were tortured and who were responsible for the decision to use torture. To prosecute would not be to criminalize policy differences, but to punish a criminal policy.

Senior Officials Should Be Investigated

The issue appears to have been debated at high highest levels of the White House if not in the Oval Office itself, and that's where responsibility should be lodged. A bipartisan Senate Armed Services Committee report concluded that "senior officials in the United States government solicited information on how to use aggressive techniques, redefined the law to create the appearance of their legality, and authorized their use against detainees."

Of course, any investigation must be impartial and nonpartisan. Moreover, assessing blame becomes tougher as one moves down the chain of command. While no one wants to accept an "I was only following orders" defense, the cases become harder where intelligence or military personnel are relying on the Justice Department, which officially baptized improper conduct. Nor should a bad legal opinion result in criminal penalties, though bad lawyering should be exposed, and anyone who knowingly relied on a bad legal opinion acted unreasonably and thus should be held accountable. An investigation first should report what happened. Then prosecution decisions should be made, taking into account the full circumstances.

The United States Has an Obligation to Prosecute

On the torture issue, at least, the administration may find it difficult not to prosecute. When [Attorney General] Eric Holder told the Senate Judiciary Committee that waterboarding was torture, he was telling the nation that the Bush administration had violated the law. Noted Jennifer Daskal of Human Rights Watch: "It would be contrary to the principles of the criminal justice system for the attorney general to say he believes a very serious crime has been committed and then to do nothing about it."

The 1949 Geneva Convention and United Nations Convention Against Torture (both ratified by the U.S.) make it even harder to avoid the case. Indeed, the latter mandates that states prosecute potential offenders or extradite them to another country for prosecution. Law professors Anthony D'Amato and Jordan J. Paust, the latter a former faculty member at the Judge Advocate General's School, argue that for this reason the president has "the duty to prosecute or extradite persons who are reasonably accused of having committed and abetted war crimes or crimes against humanity."

> **FAST FACT**
>
> A 2009 *USA Today*/Gallup poll found that two-thirds of Americans support some form of investigation to determine whether George W. Bush administration officials used torture to interrogate suspected terrorists. It also found that four in ten Americans favor criminal investigations into the matter.

The Bush administration mercifully has concluded, but its malign impact lingers. President Obama must confront the Bush legacy. He has started the process by ordering the closure of Guantanamo Bay and end of torture, but he then must turn a spotlight on his predecessor's policies, which were certainly abusive and likely illegal. And he must call to account those who implemented such policies.

Holding Lawbreakers Accountable Is Good for the Country

Yes, the process may be divisive. Yes, assessing conduct and culpability won't be easy. Yes, interrogators are likely to grow more cautious in the future. But we claim to be defending America's constitutional order of limited government and individual liberty. The Bush administration committed serious crimes. The U.S. punished its own soldiers who used such tactics against Filipino

Army major general Antonio M. Taguba, right, investigated the torture scandal at Abu Ghraib and filed a report that cited numerous "sadistic, blatant and rampant criminal abuses" at the US-run prison.

guerrillas following the Spanish-American War, as well as Japanese officers who employed the practice in World War II. *Salon* columnist Glenn Greenwald points to the Bush Justice Department's recent prosecution of the son of former Liberian President Charles Taylor for torture: "The gravity of the offense of torture is beyond dispute," opined the outgoing administration. If we merely wave good-by to those who have ostentatiously violated the law, what is to stop future law-breaking by future government officials, including against precisely these liberties?

Michael Ratner of Columbia Law School makes the obvious point that "The only way to prevent this from happening again is to make sure that those who were responsible for the torture program pay the price for it." The need for deterrence should be obvious from the fact that, notes Greenwald, "The same controversies over government law-breaking arise over and over. And why is that? Because our political leaders keep breaking the law." Deterrence is important. Greenwald, who has written extensively on this topic, points to FBI officials, among others, who refused to cooperate in the use of torture out of apparent fear of criminal sanctions. But at some point the guilty must be punished, else deterrence disappears.

No President Should Be Above the Law

Nevertheless, Washington's usual suspects have ordained that the past should be forgotten, a bit of unpleasantness to be swept under the proverbial political rug as the bright future dawns with Barack Obama's ascension to the presidency. For instance, David Ignatius of the *Washington Post* dismissed "liberal score-settlers" at a time when we should appreciate "the dangers America still faces from al-Qaeda and its allies." But no president should be immune from prosecution for breaking the law, irrespective of the challenges facing America. Dawn Johnson, the Indiana University law professor tapped to head the Office of Legal Counsel, which blessed torture early in the Bush administration, observed: "We must avoid any temptation simply to move on. We must instead be honest with ourselves and the world as we condemn our nation's past transgressions and reject Bush's corruption of our American ideals."

Put simply, moving on requires settling up. Is there a criminal defendant alive who wouldn't like to see the government drop its prosecution in the name of "moving forward"? As Robert Jackson explained in his opening address to the Nuremberg Tribunal:[1] the law must "not stop with the punishment of petty crimes by little people. It must also reach men who possess themselves of great power."

The process of settling up should be about law rather than politics. It should be conducted in sorrow rather than rancor. And it may mean far more investigation than prosecution. But the Constitution must be defended and the law enforced. By both the president and Congress. The people of America deserve no less.

---

1. Where Nazi war criminals were tried.

EVALUATING THE AUTHORS' ARGUMENTS:

Doug Bandow claims that prosecuting former US officials who broke the law is good for the country. What evidence does he support for this claim? List at least two reasons why Bandow thinks this is so. Then, state how you think David Shribman, author of the following viewpoint, would respond to this claim. List at least two pieces of evidence for Shribman's position. Finally, state with which author you ultimately agree, and why.

Viewpoint 2

US Officials Should Not Be Prosecuted for Sanctioning the Use of Torture

David Shribman

"Presidents let their predecessors be judged by the merciless jury of history, not by the temporal verdicts of courts."

It is inappropriate to prosecute US officials for sanctioning the use of torture, argues David Shribman in the following viewpoint. For one, these officials did not sanction the use of torture; rather, according to Shribman, they allowed the use of enhanced interrogation techniques, which he says do not qualify as torture and thus are not illegal. But more importantly, Shribman warns, it is bad practice for an incoming administration to prosecute an outgoing one. In his view, if a president does not like the policies of his predecessor he has the right to change them. But prosecuting former presidents sets a bad precedent that could be dangerous for American democracy. Shribman concludes the US government should spend its time and money on

David Shribman, "Look to the Future, Not the Past," *Post-Gazette* (Pittsburgh), 2009. Reprinted by permission.

the many critical issues facing the country and not waste energy trying to bring its political predecessors to justice. Shribman is executive editor of the *Post-Gazette,* Pittsburgh's daily newspaper.

AS YOU READ, CONSIDER THE FOLLOWING QUESTIONS:
1. Name at least three scenarios in which incoming presidents chose not to prosecute their outgoing predecessors, according to Shribman.
2. In Shribman's opinion, what issues are a greater priority than the prosecution of former officials? Name at least three.
3. What Winston Churchill quote is included in the viewpoint? Which of Shribman's arguments does it directly support?

When Thomas Jefferson succeeded John Adams, a contest that put America on such a different footing that it is remembered today as the Revolution of 1800, he did not seek to put members of the Adams administration on trial. When Warren G. Harding followed Woodrow Wilson in the White House in 1921, he did not put Edith Galt Wilson on trial for usurping the office of the presidency after Wilson's stroke. When Bill Clinton ended a dozen years of Republican rule in 1993, he did not try to prosecute Ronald Reagan and George H.W. Bush for deceiving the Congress over the Iran-Contra affair.[1]

In the span of 220 years there have been 43 changes of presidents, and always this rule, never written but never broken, has prevailed: Presidents let their predecessors be judged by the merciless jury of history, not by the temporal verdicts of courts.

Commentators and historians often apply a facile shorthand to describe the fundamental principle (and surpassing greatness) of the American political system: Here the transfer of power from one party to another, or from one president to another, is accomplished by ballots, not bullets. That shorthand has an unspoken corollary: Here presidents and parties do not criminalize the policies of their predecessors.

That is why the nascent effort to investigate and perhaps prosecute members of the [George W.] Bush administration is a dramatic

1. A scandal in which US officials secretly facilitated the sale of weapons to Iran, America's enemy.

departure from American tradition. It may be true that the Bush administration supported anti-terrorism policies that were deplorable, immoral—and ultimately ineffective. But is the writing of legal briefs on highly controversial, contestable and, even now, unresolved questions of law criminal?

US Officials Did Not Break the Law

This is no defense of torture nor of the tactics the Bush administration may have used in recent years; press accounts of those episodes that emerged late last month [March 2009] were shocking. But far below

Thomas Jefferson established the precedent of not prosecuting former members of presidential administrations for actions they took during their time in office.

the surface of the noisy Washington and cable-television conversation is a quieter but very serious debate, sparked by the circulation in elite legal circles in recent days of an Internet version of a forthcoming article in the *Yale Law Journal* that argues that "all interrogation methods allegedly authorized since 9/11, with the possible exception of waterboarding, have been authorized before."

This article, by William Ranney Levi, is significant as much for its intellectual provenance as it is for its contents. Mr. Levi, part of one of the most distinguished legal families in the nation, exposed his argument to the rigorous review of several leading legal minds, conservative and liberal, some of whom doubtlessly disagree with him.

He cites consultations with Jack L. Goldsmith, the conservative Harvard law professor who resigned from the Bush Justice Department and later expressed qualms over the Bush anti-terrorism legal rationale; Harold H. Koh, the dean of the Yale Law School and a leading human rights activist who has been nominated by Mr. [Barack] Obama to be legal adviser to the State Department; Mariano-Florentino Cuellar, a Stanford law professor in the Obama inner ring; and Martin S. Lederman, a Georgetown law professor and fierce Bush critic who is the president's choice for a leadership position in the powerful and prestigious Office of Legal Counsel at the Justice Department.

The meaning of all of this is not that the Bush policies were smart, prudent, moral or effective. They may not have been any of those things. The meaning, however, is that the Bush policies were legally plausible.

Presidents Do Not Prosecute Other Presidents

That almost isn't the point. The preeminent point here is that in the United States, sitting presidents and winning political parties don't

Americans Do Not Want to Pursue Prosecution

A 2009 CNN poll found that most Americans do not want to prosecute the US officials who authorized the use of harsh interrogation techniques on captured terrorists. Even more believe that the people who carried out the interrogations should not be prosecuted.

Question: "Do you think that the people who *authorized* harsh interrogation techniques should be prosecuted, or not?"

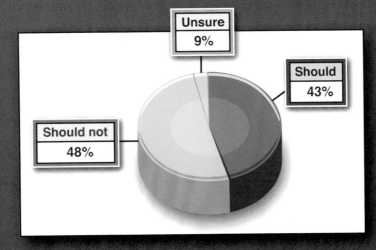

Unsure 9%

Should 43%

Should not 48%

Question: "Do you think that people who *conducted* interrogations using these techniques should be prosecuted, or not?"

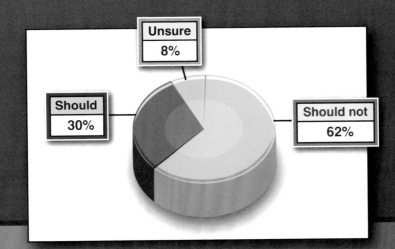

Unsure 8%

Should 30%

Should not 62%

Taken from: Ipsos/McClatchy poll conducted by Ipsos Public Affairs, April 30–May 3, 2009. N=518 adults nationwide.

sit in legal judgment of their predecessors. If they do not like their policies, and many times they do not, they change policies. They do not sue their predecessors nor seek to punish them legally. This custom has prevailed in times of severe crisis as much as in serene times.

There are myriad examples. Jimmy Carter did not seek to prosecute Henry A. Kissinger for complicity in the invasion of Cambodia and involvement in Chile, two actions that might be regarded as peculiarly subject to legal review. Richard M. Nixon did not seek to prosecute Lyndon B. Johnson for the illegal wiretapping of Martin Luther King's bathroom and bedroom, which King did not know about until [Supreme Court justice] Thurgood Marshall informed him in 1964. Nor did Nixon take any action about the illegal taping of White House conversations in the Johnson years.

We Should Not Play Tit-for-Tat Politics

In the latter two cases the explanations were political, not legal. The wiretapping of King was conducted on the authority of J. Edgar Hoover, the FBI director whom Nixon dared not alienate. He had to deal with Hoover as well, and he had his own secrets to protect, or soon would. Moreover, a man who was going to conduct his own taping in the White House was not likely to be predisposed to take legal action against taping by his predecessor.

But in this case, politics is not an insubstantial factor, perhaps for the good of the system. If the Obama team, or the Democrats acting separately from the White House, continue down the road of legal review, they will assure that their successors do the same thing once they are out of office. If you think the politics of 2009 are rough, you will shudder when you contemplate the politics of 2013 or 2017.

"You have to be very careful when and how and what you do in this arena," Democratic Sen. John F. Kerry of Massachusetts, who was separated from the presidency in 2004 by the electoral votes of only Ohio, said in a conversation the other day.

Americans Have More Pressing Issues to Address

The American system already has a set of checks and balances. It does not need another one. Nor does a president who has vowed a new bipartisanship need a legal inquisition to detract attention from his real priorities, which are his national-security challenges, the economic downturn, education, health care and climate change.

The greatest wisdom on this subject comes from an honorary American. "If the present tries to sit in judgment of the past," [former British prime minister] Winston Churchill wrote, "it will lose the future."

My guess is that Mr. Obama will call a halt to this or let the natural state of Washington prevail by sitting back and watching while the passions cool and nothing happens. About six weeks ago [March 2009] George W. Bush said that he would refrain from criticizing his successor because Mr. Obama "deserves my silence." Perhaps Mr. Obama, for the good of his own presidency and for the good of the presidency itself, will return the favor.

EVALUATING THE AUTHORS' ARGUMENTS:

David Shribman characterizes the movement to prosecute former US officials as a political matter. Doug Bandow, author of the previous viewpoint, characterizes the movement to prosecute former officials as a legal matter. Explain the difference between these two characterizations. Then, state with which author's perspective you agree? Do you think the use of enhanced interrogation tactics is ultimately a political or legal matter? Explain your reasoning.

Viewpoint
3

The United States Should Apply the Geneva Conventions to Terrorists

Steven R. Ratner

"In losing sight of the crucial protections of the conventions, the United States invites a world of wars in which laws disappear."

Steven R. Ratner is a law professor at the University of Michigan. In the following viewpoint he argues the Geneva Conventions—decades-old rules about how nations must treat prisoners of war—ought to be applied to terrorists. Although terrorists do not fight for any nation or formal body, and the war on terror is a non-traditional type of war, Ratner says that terrorists and other enemy combatants are nonetheless covered by the conventions. In fact, Article 3 of the conventions protects all persons regardless of their status and regardless of the type of war being fought, he says. He also points out that the Geneva Conventions have historically covered non-traditional war actors, and terrorists are no different. Ratner believes operating outside the Geneva Conventions invites a type of

Steven R. Ratner, "Think Again: Geneva Conventions," *Foreign Policy,* March 1, 2008. Reprinted by permission.

chaos and lawlessness that would shock even the most war-weary peoples. He urges the United States to apply the Geneva Conventions to terrorists to safeguard its own reputation and to maintain an important standard of decency in warfare.

AS YOU READ, CONSIDER THE FOLLOWING QUESTIONS:
1. What are Vietcong guerrillas and how do they factor into the author's argument?
2. According to Ratner, what did the Supreme Court declare in 2006?
3. What kinds of interrogation tactics does Ratner say are allowable under the Geneva Conventions?

The laws of armed conflict are old; they date back millennia to warrior codes used in ancient Greece. But the modern Geneva Conventions, which govern the treatment of soldiers and civilians in war, can trace their direct origin to 1859, when Swiss businessman Henri Dunant happened upon the bloody aftermath of the Battle of Solferino. His outrage at the suffering of the wounded led him to establish what would become the International Committee of the Red Cross, which later lobbied for rules improving the treatment of injured combatants. Decades later, when the devastation of World War II demonstrated that broader protections were necessary, the modern Geneva Conventions were created, producing a kind of international "bill of rights" that governs the handling of casualties, prisoners of war (POWs), and civilians in war zones. Today, the conventions have been ratified by every nation on the planet.

The Geneva Conventions Remain Relevant

Of course, the drafters probably never imagined a conflict like the war on terror or combatants like al Qaeda. The conventions were always primarily concerned with wars between states. That can leave some of the protections enshrined in the laws feeling a little old-fashioned today. It seems slightly absurd to worry too much about captured terrorists' tobacco rations or the fate of a prisoner's horse, as the conventions do. So, when then White House Counsel Alberto Gonzales wrote President George W. Bush in 2002 arguing that the "new paradigm" of armed conflict rendered parts of the conventions "obsolete" and "quaint," he had a point. In very specific—and minor—details, the conventions have been superseded by time and technology.

But the core provisions and, more crucially, the spirit of the conventions remain enormously relevant for modern warfare. For one, the world is still home to dozens of wars, for which the conventions have important, unambiguous rules, such as forbidding pillaging and prohibiting the use of child soldiers. These rules apply to both aggressor and defending nations, and, in civil wars, to governments and insurgent groups.

FAST FACT

The United States has ratified all of the Geneva Conventions, except for two that were added in 1977. These relate to the protection of victims of international and internal conflicts.

The conventions won't prevent wars—they were never intended to—but they can and do protect innocent bystanders, shield soldiers from unnecessary harm, limit the physical damage caused by war, and even enhance the chances for cease-fires and peace. The fundamental bedrock of the conventions is to prevent suffering in war, and that gives them a legitimacy for anyone touched by conflict, anywhere and at any time. That is hardly quaint or old-fashioned.

The Geneva Conventions Apply to al Qaeda

The Bush administration's position since Sept. 11, 2001, has been that the global war on terror is a different kind of war, one in which the Geneva Conventions do not apply. It is true that the laws do not specifically mention wars against nonstate actors such as al Qaeda. But there have always been "irregular" forces that participate in warfare, and the conflicts of the 20th century were no exception. The French Resistance during World War II operated without uniforms. Vietcong guerrillas fighting in South Vietnam were not part of any formal army, but the United States nonetheless treated those they captured as POWs.

So what treatment should al Qaeda get? The conventions contain one section—Article 3—that protects all persons regardless of their status, whether spy, mercenary, or terrorist, and regardless of the type of war in which they are fighting. That same article prohibits torture, cruel treatment, and murder of all detainees, requires the wounded to be cared for, and says that any trials must be conducted by regular courts respecting due process. In a landmark 2006 opinion, the U.S. Supreme Court declared that at a minimum Article 3 applies to detained al Qaeda suspects. In other words, the rules apply, even if al Qaeda ignores them.

And it may be that even tougher rules should be used in such a fight. Many other governments, particularly in Europe, believe that

The modern Geneva Conventions govern the treatment of soldiers. Their origin can be traced to Swiss businessman and founder of the International Red Cross Henri Dunant.

a "war" against terror—a war without temporal or geographic limits—is complete folly, insisting instead that the fight against terrorist groups should be a law enforcement, not a military, matter. For decades, Europe has prevented and punished terrorists by treating them as criminals. Courts in Britain and Spain have tried suspects for major bombings in London and Madrid. The prosecutors and investigators there did so while largely complying with obligations enshrined in human rights treaties, which constrain them far more than do the Geneva Conventions. . . .

Interrogations of Terrorists Are Perfectly Legal

If you've seen a classic war movie such as *The Great Escape*, you know that prisoners of war are only obligated to provide name, rank, date of birth, and military serial number to their captors. But the Geneva Conventions do not ban interrogators from asking for more. In fact, the laws were written with the expectation that states will grill prisoners, and clear rules were created to manage the process. In interstate war, any form of coercion is forbidden, specifically threats, insults, or punishments if prisoners fail to answer; for all other wars, cruel or degrading treatment and torture are prohibited. But questioning detainees is perfectly legal; it simply must be done in a manner that respects human dignity. The conventions thus hardly require rolling out the red carpet for suspected terrorists. Many interrogation tactics are clearly allowed, including good cop–bad cop scenarios, repetitive or rapid questioning, silent periods, and playing to a detainee's ego.

The Bush administration has engaged in legal gymnastics to avoid the conventions' restrictions, arguing that preventing the next attack is sufficient rationale for harsh tactics such as waterboarding, sleep deprivation, painful stress positions, deafening music, and traumatic humiliation. These severe methods have been used despite the protests of a growing chorus of intelligence officials who say that such approaches are actually counterproductive to extracting quality information. Seasoned interrogators consistently say that straightforward questioning is far more successful for getting at the truth. So, by mangling the conventions, the United States has joined the company of a host of unsavory regimes that make regular use of torture. It has abandoned a system that protects U.S. military personnel from terrible treatment for one in which the rules are made on the fly. . . .

Without the Geneva Conventions, Horror and Chaos

It is enormously important that the United States reaffirms its commitment to the conventions, for the sake of the country's reputation and that of the conventions. Those who rely on the flawed logic that because al Qaeda does not treat the conventions seriously, neither should the United States fail to see not only the chaos the world will suffer in exchange for these rules; they also miss the fact that the United States will have traded basic rights and protections harshly learned through thousands of years of war for the nitpicking decisions of a small group of partisan lawyers huddled in secret. Rather than advancing U.S. interests by following an established standard of behavior in this new type of war, the United States—and any country that chooses to abandon these hard-won rules—risks basing its policies on narrow legalisms. In losing sight of the crucial protections of the conventions, the United States invites a world of wars in which laws disappear. And the horrors of such wars would far surpass anything the war on terror could ever deliver.

EVALUATING THE AUTHORS' ARGUMENTS:

Both Steven R. Ratner and J.B. Williams (author of the following viewpoint) think that nothing less than the downfall of US society is at stake in the war on terror. Yet Ratner thinks failure to extend the Geneva Conventions to terrorists will contribute to this downfall. Williams, on the other hand, believes extending the conventions to terrorists will contribute to this downfall. After reading both viewpoints, with which author do you agree? Why? Explain your reasoning and quote from each text in your answer.

Viewpoint
4

The Geneva Conventions Should Not Be Applied to Terrorists

J.B. Williams

"International terrorists do NOT meet any of the conditions stated in the Geneva Convention[s]."

In the following viewpoint, J.B. Williams argues the Geneva Conventions do not apply to terrorists. He explains that terrorists meet none of the conditions of the Geneva Conventions, such as being members of a nation that has signed the conventions, or being part of a militia that has a well-defined chain of command. In addition, terrorists do not carry their weapons openly, nor do they take pains to distinguish themselves from civilians—in fact, terrorists often hide among civilians when they fight, and strive to include civilians in the body count of their attacks. For all of these reasons, Williams says, these types of warriors should not be afforded protection under the conventions. Williams concludes that extending civilized protection to fighters who would not reciprocate such treatment puts the United States at a grave disadvantage in this most crucial

J.B. Williams, "Terrorism, Security and Geneva," *Canada Free Press,* 2006. Reprinted by permission.

conflict. Williams is a political commentator whose articles have appeared in the *Canada Free Press,* where this viewpoint was originally published.

AS YOU READ, CONSIDER THE FOLLOWING QUESTIONS:
1. What four conditions does Williams say combatants must meet if they are to be protected by the Geneva Conventions?
2. List at least two ways in which international terrorists do not meet Geneva Conventions conditions, according to Williams.
3. What, according to Williams, is the harm in "playing nice" to terrorists?

Secretary of Defense [Donald] Rumsfeld is under fire for allegedly sanctioning inhumane detention and interrogation policies concerning captured terrorists. This claim is based on a number of well publicized incidents and assumes that international terrorists are party to and covered by The Geneva Convention[s]. It also assumes some ambiguous definitions of inhumane treatments. . . .

Somewhere along the way, one concerned with such matters must consider the facts and make valued judgments on the basis of the evidence and facts as they exist. When discussing such a serious charge with severe penalties, one has a responsibility to know and act upon facts, not politically driven rhetoric aimed at undermining the war effort itself.

If it's true that all Americans want proper national defense measures while enforcing and adhering to humane treatment of enemy captives, then we must begin with knowing what the Geneva Convention[s] says, who it applies to (and doesn't), be honest in the assessment of events and apply the same rules of engagement expected of ourselves, to enemy forces. . . .

Terrorists Are Not Covered by the Geneva Conventions

The Geneva Convention(s) is a negotiated agreement between signer nations who have voluntarily agreed to abide by and therefore be protected by the terms of this agreement. Voluntary signer nations should expect to benefit from these protections, so long as they abide by

The Geneva Conventions were signed by participating countries on December 13, 1949.

these protections themselves. Non-signer nations have NOT agreed to abide by these terms and are therefore, not protected by these terms. It is that simple.

Combatants from signer nations are obligated under this agreement to meet certain conditions in order to be protected by this agreement. Specifically, protected combatants are defined as follows. . . .

- members of the armed forces of a party to an international conflict,
- members of militias or volunteer corps including members of organized resistance movements as long as they have a well-defined chain of command,
- are clearly distinguishable from the civilian population,
- carry their arms openly, and obey the laws of war

Combatants do not have to meet one of these conditions in order to receive protection under the Geneva Convention(s), they must meet ALL of them. The Convention(s) goes on to state clearly, *"However other individuals, including civilians, who commit hostile acts and are captured do not have these protections."*

Terrorists Defy All Geneva Conventions Criteria

International terrorists do NOT meet any of the conditions stated in the Geneva Convention[s] in order to gain protection as a known enemy combatant. They do NOT serve in any organized armed force serving any particular nation. They do NOT have any well-defined chain of command or control. They go out of their way to be indistinguishable from the civilian population and have gone so far as to disguise themselves as medical, police and press personnel. They do NOT carry arms openly or obey any set of laws. They distinguish between military and civilian targets only to the degree that they prefer attacking unarmed defenseless civilian targets as opposed to military targets. As such, they are NOT covered by the language or terms of the Geneva Convention(s).

Where's the confusion? As with any confusion concerning any law, the confusion comes through interpretation of the law. On June 29, 2006, The US Supreme Court issued a ruling in the *Hamdan v. Rumsfeld* case. This decision is 185 pages long. The question of whether or not Hamdan was to be protected as a "prisoner of war" as defined by the Geneva Convention[s], required a 185 page answer. That alone should tell you something. The decision is typical of rulings by today's Supreme Court. It is more of a non-decision than a decision, which is why it took 185 pages to explain its non-decision.

FAST FACT

No terrorist organization, such as al Qaeda, Hamas, or Hezbollah, has ever signed or indicated a desire to sign the Geneva Conventions.

Putting Ourselves at a Disadvantage

Why would we offer Geneva Convention[s] protections to terrorists? To begin with, most of us wouldn't. Most of those who would, have never read the Geneva Convention(s), and many others would demand humane treatment of even the most inhumane enemies under the heading of "do unto others", as if playing nice will cause our enemies to play nice.

We are not talking about prisoners of war, serving a signer nations government under a distinct chain of command, obligated to abide by the same rules of engagement we are willing to abide by. We are talking about terrorists. People (to use the term loosely) who hide behind

Signatories of the Geneva Conventions

More than two hundred countries have signed the Geneva Conventions, which require prisoners of war to be treated humanely. No terrorist group or other nonnational entity is a signatory to the treaty.

The countries of the world that have ratified the conventions

The countries of the world that have not ratified the conventions but are covered by some other country

The countries of the world that have not ratified the conventions and are NOT covered by some other country

civilian women and children in a constant effort to attack unarmed civilian targets for purpose of creating terror in the hearts and minds of innocents in pursuit of tyrannical rule by the bloodiest of means.

They do not abide by any rules of engagement at all and won't no matter how much we hamstring our own troops in their efforts to defend innocent civilians seeking peace and security.

Nobody sanctioned the sexual misconduct of a few at Abu Ghraib prison.[1] Our detainees are not beheaded or dismembered—they are

1. Where US soldiers abused Iraqi prisoners of war.

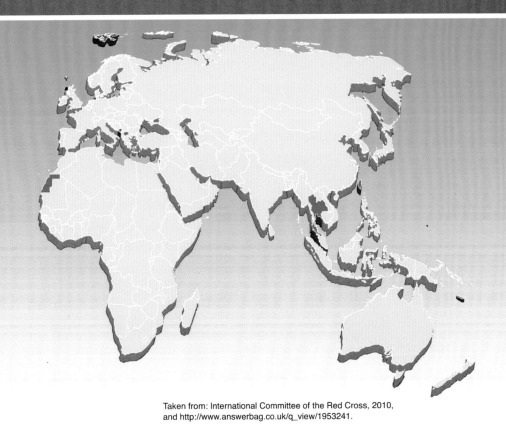

Taken from: International Committee of the Red Cross, 2010, and http://www.answerbag.co.uk/q_view/1953241.

not dragged through the streets behind SUV's or burned to death before cameras for perverted public consumption. But our soldiers and civilians are and that's why we must not forget who our enemy is, what he is willing to do and what life will be like for all, it we fail to eliminate this particular enemy.

Terrorists Should Not Benefit from Our Civility

Today, innocent Iraqi citizens are dying, not at the hands of American or coalition forces, or at the hands of so-called "insurgents", but rather at the hands of terrorists, referred to by many as simple "insurgents".

But many of these so-called "insurgents" are not from Iraq and do not have any stake in Iraq's future. They have a deep seated opposition to and hatred for western democratic values. And if they were not attacking innocents in Iraq, they would be attacking innocents in many places around the globe, including America.

So before we afford these terrorists Geneva Conventio[s] protections or American civil rights, make it a point to know the facts and consider the consequences of that decision. Contrary to the rhetoric surrounding the subject, we are very much talking the life or death of thousands here. The stakes can't get any higher.

EVALUATING THE AUTHORS' ARGUMENTS:

J.B. Williams argues that since al Qaeda terrorists do not follow or respect the Geneva Conventions, the United States should not apply the Geneva rules to them. How does Steven R. Ratner, author of the previous viewpoint, directly respond to this argument? After explaining Ratner's position, state with which author you ultimately agree, and why.

Facts About Torture

Editor's note: These facts can be used in reports to add credibility when making important points or claims.

The Convention Against Torture and Other Cruel, Inhuman, or Degrading Treatment or Punishment is an international anti-torture document first opened for signature at the United Nations on February 4, 1985.

It consists of thirty-three articles that articulate the following statements and procedures regarding torture:
- Defines torture as any act that inflicts intentional physical or mental pain or suffering for the purpose of obtaining information, confessions, or inflicting punishment.
- Each signatory will take all measures to prevent acts of torture in its territories.
- War, the threat of war, public emergencies, or other catastrophic situations may not be used to justify torture.
- Officers or officials may not order their subordinates to torture; likewise, an order from a superior may not be used to justify the use of torture.
- No signatory may extradite a person to another state where it is likely he will be tortured.
- Each signatory will treat acts of torture as criminal offenses that will be assigned appropriate punishments.
- Signatories will make sure that law enforcement personnel, civil or military, medical personnel, public officials and other persons who may be involved in the custody, interrogation or treatment of any individual subjected to any form of arrest, detention or imprisonment be educated about the prohibition against torture.
- Each State Party shall keep under systematic review interrogation rules, instructions, methods and practices as well as arrangements

for the custody and treatment of persons subjected to any form of arrest, detention or imprisonment in any territory under its jurisdiction, with a view to preventing any cases of torture.
- Signatories will investigate responsible parties when there are grounds to believe torture has been used.
- Signatories will appropriately investigate claims of torture and make sure their legal systems can appropriately defend and compensate victims of torture.
- An international Committee Against Torture, consisting of ten experts on human rights, will be formed to enforce these provisions.

Global Opinions About Torture
A 2008 World Public Opinion.org poll of more than 19,000 citizens of 19 different countries found the following regarding opinions about torture:

On average across all nations polled:
- 57 percent of the public supports unequivocal rules that ban torture.
- 26 percent favors limited use of torture in order to save innocent lives.
- 9 percent thinks torture should be generally allowed.

In 14 of the 19 countries, the majority of citizens favors an unequivocal ban on torture:

- In Spain, 82 percent of the public supports such a ban.
- In Great Britain, 82 percent supports such a ban.
- In France, 82 percent supports such a ban.
- In Mexico, 73 percent supports such a ban.
- In China, 66 percent supports such a ban.
- In the Palestinian Territories, 66 percent supports such a ban.
- In Poland, 62 percent supports such a ban.
- In Indonesia, 61 percent supports such a ban.
- In Ukraine, 59 percent of the public supports such a ban.
- In Azerbaijan, 54 percent supports such a ban.
- In Egypt, 54 percent supports such a ban.
- In the United States, 53 percent supports such a ban.

- In Russia, 49 percent supports such a ban.
- In Iran, 43 percent supports such a ban.

The citizens above support an outright ban on torture even if torturing a terrorist would prevent a terrorist attack and save innocent lives.

Large majorities of people in all 19 nations favor a general prohibition against torture.

In all nations polled, less than 1 in 5 people said that their government should generally be able to use torture.

In 4 countries, a majority of citizens favor allowing torture to be used in the event a terrorist has information about an impending attack and torturing the terrorist could reveal information that would save innocent lives. They are:

- India (59 percent supported such an exception)
- Nigeria (54 percent supported such an exception)
- Turkey (51 percent supported such an exception)
- Thailand (44 percent supported such an exception)

The following nations had the largest percentages of citizens who think torture should be generally allowed:

- China (18 percent)
- Turkey (18 percent)
- Nigeria (15 percent)
- South Korea (13 percent)
- United States (13 percent)
- India (12 percent)
- Thailand (10 percent)

Organizations to Contact

The editors have compiled the following list of organizations concerned with the issues debated in this book. The descriptions are derived from materials provided by the organizations. All have publications or information available for interested readers. The list was compiled on the date of publication of the present volume; the information provided here may change. Be aware that many organizations take several weeks or longer to respond to inquiries, so allow as much time as possible for the receipt of requested materials.

American Civil Liberties Union (ACLU)
125 Broad St., 18th Fl.
New York, NY 10004-2400
(212) 549-2500
e-mail: aclu@aclu.org
website: www.aclu.org

The ACLU works to defend Americans' civil rights guaranteed by the US Constitution. Following the September 2001 terrorist attacks, the ACLU founded its National Security Project, which litigates national security cases involving discrimination, torture, detention, surveillance, and secrecy, to protect every human's fundamental rights. The group's website has an entire section devoted to the subject of torture.

Amnesty International USA (AI USA)
5 Penn Plaza
New York, NY 10001
(212) 807-8400
website: www.amnesty-usa.org

AI USA is a global organization that works toward fair and prompt trials for political prisoners and an end to torture and executions.

Center for Defense Information (CDI)
1779 Massachusetts Ave. NW, Ste. 615
Washington, DC 20036
(202) 332-0600

fax: (202) 462-4559
e-mail: into@cdi.org
website: www.cdi.org

CDI is a nonpartisan, nonprofit organization that researches all aspects of global security. It seeks to educate the public and policy makers about issues such as nuclear weapons, security policy, and terrorist threats through its numerous programs, including Homeland Defense, Terrorism, and Nuclear Proliferation to name a few.

Center for Strategic and International Studies (CSIS)
1800 K St. NW
Washington, DC 20006
(202) 887-0200
fax: (202) 775-3199
e-mail: webmaster@csis.org
website: www.csis.org

CSIS is a bipartisan public policy think tank that focuses on America's economic policy, national security, and foreign and domestic policies. The center conducts research and provides strategic insight and policy solutions for government decision makers. It produces ample reports about national security and terrorism.

Department of Homeland Security (DHS)
US Department of Homeland Security
Washington, DC 20528
(202) 282-8000
website: www.dhs.gov

The DHS was created after the September 11, 2001, terrorist attacks. The department serves to secure the nation while preserving American freedoms and liberties. It is charged with protecting the United States from terrorists, decreasing the country's vulnerability to terrorism, and effectively responding to attacks. The current DHS homeland security strategic plan can be found on its website.

Federal Bureau of Investigation (FBI)
935 Pennsylvania Ave., NW
Washington, DC 20535-000

(202) 324-3000

website: www.fbi.gov

The FBI works hand in hand with law enforcement agencies, intelligence organizations, the military, and diplomatic circles to neutralize terrorist cells and operatives in the United States and to dismantle terrorist networks worldwide.

Human Rights First

333 Seventh Ave., 13th Fl.

New York, NY 10001-5108

(212) 845-5200

website: www.humanrightsfirst.org

This nonprofit human rights organization opposes the use of enhanced interrogation techniques by the US government or any other entity. It was originally founded in 1978 as the Lawyers Committee for International Human Rights to promote laws and policies that advance universal rights and freedoms.

Human Rights Watch

350 Fifth Avenue, 34th Fl.

New York, NY 10118-3299

(212) 290-4700

fax: (212) 736-1300

e-mail: hrwnyc@hrw.org · website: www.hrw.org

Human Rights Watch is an independent organization that regularly investigates human rights abuses in over seventy countries around the world and holds violators of these rights accountable. It works to lay the legal and moral groundwork to defend and protect human rights for all while also promoting civil liberties and defending freedom of thought, due process, and equal protection of the law. It publishes the Human Rights Watch Quarterly newsletter and the annual Human Rights Watch World Report.

International Policy Institute for Counter-Terrorism (ICT)

PO Box 167, Herzlia, 46150, Israel

972-9-9527277

fax: 972-9-9513073

e-mail: info@ict.org.il
website: www.ict.org.il

This research institute develops public policy solutions to international terrorism. Its website is a comprehensive resource on terrorism and counterterrorism, including an extensive database on terrorist organizations.

International Rehabilitation Council for Torture Victims (IRCT)
Borgergade 13
PO Box 9049
1022 Copenhagen K Denmark
e-mail: irct@irct.org
website: www.irct.org
IRCT is the umbrella organization for more than 140 independent torture rehabilitation organizations in over seventy countries. Each year its members treat more than one hundred thousand torture survivors and their families.

National Counterterrorism Center (NCTC)
website: www.nctc.gov

The NCTC is charged with analyzing terrorism intelligence, storing terrorism information, and providing lists of terrorists, terrorist groups, and worldwide terrorist incidents to the intelligence community. The NCTC also writes assessments and briefings for policy makers. The NCTC's Press Room contains press releases, interviews, speeches and testimony, fact sheets, and published reports, as well as the legislation that guides the center's actions.

National Religious Campaign Against Torture (NRCAT)
110 Maryland Ave. NE, Ste. 502
Washington, DC 20002
(202) 547-1920
e-mail: campaign@nrcat.org
website: www.nrcat.org

This organization was started in January 2006. It is a coalition of more than 290 religious groups, including members who are Roman Catholic, evangelical Christian, mainline Protestant, Unitarian, Quaker, Orthodox Christian, Jewish, Muslim, Baha'i, Buddhist, Hindu and Sikh. Together they are committed to ending US-sponsored and US-enabled torture, and cruel, inhuman, and degrading treatment.

National Security Agency (NSA)
9800 Savage Rd.
Ft. George Meade, MD 20755
(301) 688-6524
fax: (301) 688-6198
website: www.nsa.gov

The NSA is a cryptologic agency administered by the US Department of Defense. Its main goal is to protect national security systems and to produce foreign intelligence information. The NSA follows US laws to defeat terrorist organizations at home and abroad and ensures the protection of privacy and civil liberties of American citizens. Speeches, congressional testimonies, press releases, and research reports are all available on the NSA website.

US Department of Justice (DOJ)
950 Pennsylvania Ave. NW
Washington, DC 20530-0001
(202) 514-2000
e-mail: AskDOJ@usdoj.gov
website: www.usdoj.gov

The DOJ functions to enforce the law and defend the interests of the United States. Its primary duties are to ensure public safety against foreign and domestic threats; to provide federal leadership in preventing and controlling crime; to seek just punishment for those guilty of unlawful behavior; to administer and enforce US immigration laws fairly and effectively; and to ensure fair and impartial administration of justice for all Americans.

For Further Reading

Books

Matthew Alexander and John Bruning, *How to Break a Terrorist: The U.S. Interrogators Who Used Brains, Not Brutality, to Take Down the Deadliest Man in Iraq.* New York: Free Press, 2008. This book, cowritten by an air force officer, tells how intelligence forces located and killed Abu Musab Al Zarqawi, the head of al Qaeda in Iraq.

Bob Brecher, *Torture and the Ticking Bomb.* New York: Wiley-Blackwell, 2007. Argues that even torture for a seemingly good cause—such as to extract information from a terrorist who knows where and when a bomb will strike—is counterproductive.

David Cole, ed., *Torture Memos: Rationalizing the Unthinkable.* New York: New Press, 2009. A prominent legal scholar offers readers an unfiltered look at the tactics approved for use in the CIA's secret overseas prisons.

Mark P. Donnelly and Daniel Diehl, *The Big Book of Pain: Torture & Punishment Through History.* Charleston, SC: History Press, 2011. Explores the systematic use throughout the ages of various means of punishment, torture, coercion and torment, and questions why such practices have continued for so long.

Darius Rejali, *Torture and Democracy.* Princeton, NJ: Princeton University Press, 2009. Argues that democracies like those in Great Britain and the United States, rather than despots, are actually the originators of modern torture techniques.

Philippe Sands, *Torture Team: Rumsfeld's Memo and the Betrayal of American Values.* New York: Palgrave Macmillan, 2008. Explores how enhanced interrogation policies devised by the George W. Bush administration were approved for use.

Justine Sharrock, *Tortured: When Good Soldiers Do Bad Things.* New York: Wiley, 2010. Goes behind the scenes of America's torture program through the personal stories of four American soldiers. Argues that whenever torture is used, the torturers suffer too.

Marc A. Thiessen, *Courting Disaster: How the CIA Kept America Safe and How Barack Obama Is Inviting the Next Attack.* Washington, DC: Regnery, 2010. Argues that the use of enhanced interrogation techniques have helped US intelligence officials thwart terrorist plots, and warns that dismantling this program will encourage another terrorist attack on America.

Periodicals and Internet Sources

Matthew Alexander, "I'm Still Tortured by What I Saw in Iraq," *Washington Post*, November 30, 2008. www.washingtonpost.com/wp-dyn/content/article/2008/11/28/AR2008112802242.html?hpid=opinionsbox1.

Amnesty International, "Execution by Lethal Injection: A Quarter Century of State Killing," 2007. www.amnestyusa.org/document.php?lang=e&id=engact500072007.

Julian E. Barnes and Greg Miller, "Detainee Says He Lied to CIA in Harsh Interrogations," *Los Angeles Times*, June 16, 2009. http://articles.latimes.com/2009/jun/16/nation/na-cia-detainee16.

Nick Baumann, "The Case of the Missing Torture Documents," *Mother Jones*, September 28, 2009. http://motherjones.com/politics/2009/09/case-missing-torture-documents.

Carolyn Patty Blum, Lisa Magarrell, Marieke Wierda, "Prosecuting Abuses of Detainees in U.S. Counter-Terrorism Operations," International Center for Transitional Justice, November 2009. www.ictj.org/static/Publications/ICTJ_USA_CriminalJustCriminalPolicy_pb2009.pdf.

"Botched Executions," *New York Times*, October 3, 2009. www.nytimes.com/2009/10/03/opinion/03sat2.html?_r=1.

Shmuley Boteach, "The Death Penalty for Terrorists," *Jerusalem Post*, July 21, 2008. www.jpost.com/servlet/Satellite?cid=1215331047048&pagename=JPArticle%2FShowFull.

A.J. DiCintio, "Headlines, Torture, and American Values," RenewAmerica.com, May 7, 2009. www.renewamerica.com/columns/dicintio/090507.

Aaron Emery, "Water Boarding and the Future State of Torture," Campaign for Liberty, July 3, 2009. www.campaignforliberty.com/article.php?view=110.

Dan Froomkin, "Krauthammer's Asterisks," *Washington Post*, May 1, 2009. http://voices.washingtonpost.com/white-house-watch/torture/krauthammers-asterisks.html.

Gene Healy, "Of Course It Was Torture," *Washington Examiner*, April 21, 2009. www.washingtonexaminer.com/opinion/columns/GeneHealy/Of-Course-It-Was-Torture-43285722.html.

Stanley Howard, "No Humane Way to Kill," *Socialist Worker*, May 13, 2008. http://socialistworker.org/2008/05/13/no-humane-way-to-kill.

Gary Kamiya, "America's Necessary Dark Night of the Soul," Salon.com, May 1, 2009. www.salon.com/news/opinion/kamiya/2009/05/01/torture_investigations.

Gary Kamiya, "Torture Works Sometimes—But It's Always Wrong," Salon.com, April 23, 2009. www.salon.com/news/opinion/kamiya/2009/04/23/torture.

David Kaye, "The Torture Commission We Really Need," *Foreign Policy*, March 25, 2010. www.foreignpolicy.com/articles/2010/03/25/the_torture_commission_we_really_need?page=0.1.

Charles Krauthammer, "Torture Foes Put on a Cowardly Spectacle," *New York Daily News*, May 1, 2009. www.nydailynews.com/opinions/2009/05/01/2009-05-01_torture_foes_put_on_a_cowardly_spectacle.html.

Charles Krauthammer, "Torture Foes Twist the Truth: Ticking Time Bomb Scenarios Are Real," *New York Daily News*, May 14, 2009. www.nydailynews.com/opinions/2009/05/15/2009-05-15_torture_foes_twist_the_truth.html.

Clifford D. May, "Interrogation Tactics Weren't Torture, American Officials Shouldn't Be Prosecuted," *U.S. News and World Report*, May 18, 2009. http://politics.usnews.com/opinion/articles/2009/05/18/interrogation-tactics-werent-torture-american-officials-shouldnt-be-prosecuted.html.

Anish Mitra, "The Case for Waterboarding," *Brown Spectator*, February 20, 2008. http://thebrownspectator.com/waterboarding-not-torture/.

Malcolm Nance, "Waterboarding Is Torture . . . Period," *Small Wars Journal*, October 31, 2007. http://smallwarsjournal.com/blog/2007/10/waterboarding-is-torture-perio/.

John Peeler, "Torture Memos: Don't Prosecute, But Change Law," *LA Progressive*, April 23, 2009. www.laprogressive.com/the-middle-east/torture-memos-dont-prosecute-but-change-law/.

Physicians for Human Rights, "Broken Laws, Broken Lives," June 2008. http://brokenlives.info/?page-id=69.

Jon Reinsch, "Torture and the Bomb," *Foreign Policy in Focus*, October 21, 2009. www.fpif.org/articles/torture_and_the_bomb.

Ali Soufan, "My Tortured Decision," *New York Times*, April 22, 2009. www.nytimes.com/2009/04/23/opinion/23soufan.html.

Aryeh Spero, "It's Not Torture and It Is Necessary," *Human Events*, January 16, 2007. www.humanevents.com/article.php?id=18949.

Clive Stafford Smith, "A Green Light for Torture," *Guardian* (London), February 15, 2010. www.guardian.co.uk/commentisfree/2010/feb/15/targetting-mi5-policy-makers.

Robert F. Turner, "What Went Wrong?: Torture and the Office of Legal Counsel in the Bush Administration," Testimony Before the US Senate Committee on the Judiciary Subcommittee on Administrative Oversight and the Courts, May 13, 2009. http://judiciary.senate.gov/pdf/09-05-13Turnertestimony.pdf.

Stuart Wheeler, "Torture is NEVER justified . . . and Our Spineless Leaders Must Find the Courage to Tell That to Bush," *Daily Mail* (UK), June 9, 2007. www.dailymail.co.uk/news/article-461016/Torture-NEVER-justified--spineless-leaders-courage-tell-Bush.html.

Andy Worthington, "Abu Zubaydah and the Case Against Torture Architect James Mitchell," *Eurasia Review*, June 25, 2010. www.eurasiareview.com/201006253872/abu-zubaydah-and-the-case-against-torture-architect-james-mitchell.html.

John Yoo and Glen Sulmasy, "Terrorists Are Not POWs," *FrontPage Magazine*, August 10, 2006. http://97.74.65.51/readArticle.aspx?ARTID=3130.

Websites

Campaign Against Torture (http://physiciansforhumanrights.org/torture/). This site, sponsored by the group Physicians for Human Rights was begun when allegations of torture were first made about detainees at Abu Ghraib Prison in Iraq and at Guantánamo Bay. The site's "News and Reports" section contains updated news and information related to the subject.

European Committee for the Prevention of Torture and Inhuman or Degrading Treatment or Punishment (CPT) (www.cpt.coe.int/en/default.htm). This group organizes visits to places of detention, in order to assess how persons deprived of their liberty are treated. Its website contains a useful database of all CPT reports and assessments.

The Geneva Conventions of 1949 and Their Additional Protocols (www.icrc.org/eng/war-and-law/treaties-customary-law/geneva-conventions/index.jsp). This site, maintained by the International Committee of the Red Cross, offers the full text of the Geneva Conventions. Useful for students seeking primary source materials.

National Security Archive (www.gwu.edu/~nsarchiv/index.html). This is an independent nongovernmental research institute and library located at the George Washington University. It collects and publishes declassified documents obtained through the Freedom of Information Act. Contains key documents related to the subject of torture, including the Bybee Memo.

The Torture Report (www.thetorturereport.org/). This website, maintained by the American Civil Liberties Union's National Security Project, pulls information from government documents, press reports, independent investigations, witness statements, and other publications that have reported on George W. Bush administration decisions on treatment of war on terror detainees.

United Nations Treaty Collection (http://treaties.un.org/). The full text of many key documents, including the Convention Against Torture, is available here.

Waterboarding.org (http://waterboarding.org/). This website offers a thorough description of waterboarding and a discussion of whether the practice counts as torture. Especially useful are firsthand accounts of people who had waterboarded others and been waterboarded themselves.

Index

Picture Credits